# Trusting in the Dark

# Trusting in the Dark

Kristi Holl

Illustrated by
Janice Skivington

STANDARD PUBLISHING
Cincinnati, Ohio 24-03969

*The Julie McGregor Books*

*Two of a Kind*
*Trusting in the Dark*

**Library of Congress Cataloging-in-Publication Data**

Holl, Kristi.
Trusting in the dark / by Kristi Holl, illustrated by Janice Skivington.
p. cm. -- (The Julie McGregor books)
Summary: Sixth grader Julie dislikes the sacrifices she has to make to ease her family's serious financial problems, which may cause them to lose their farm, but her faith in God helps her through the situation.
ISBN 0-87403-749-2
[1. Money--Fiction. 2. Farm life--Fiction. 3. Christian life--Fiction.] I. Skivington, Janice, ill. II. Title. III. Series: Holl, Kristi. Julie McGregor books.
PZ7.H7079Tr 1990
[Fic]--dc 20 90-40119
CIP
AC


Published by The STANDARD PUBLISHING Company, Cincinnati, Ohio.
A division of STANDEX INTERNATIONAL Corporation.
Printed in U.S.A.

for my nephew, Michael

# *Contents*

*Chapter 1*

# The Threat

Julie McGregor hopped off the school bus and waited until it disappeared over the hill in a dusty cloud. Then, with a grin, she dropped her books beside the driveway and cartwheeled three times across the yard.

"Not bad," she congratulated herself. She brushed bits of dried leaves and twigs from her waist-length blonde hair.

Grabbing her denim book bag, she slung it over her shoulder and scuffed through the crunchy piles of October leaves. Head down, she chanted all the cheers that she'd learned for the tryouts.

Her stomach lurched as she considered the tryouts for basketball cheerleader just three weeks away. Julie had worked hard to learn the cheers and was confident that

she'd do her best at the tryouts. Whether her "best" would be good enough, well, she'd know before long.

"V! I-C! T-O! R-Y!" she shouted. "Split that V! Dot that I! Curve that C-T-O-R-Y!"

Jumping in the air, Julie whacked her leg with her book bag. With a groan she rubbed her thigh and waved to her little sister on the swing set.

"Fired up! Fired up!" Julie chanted at the back door, shooting her arms overhead. She stepped around the pumpkins squatted by the back step and opened the door, dumping her book bag on the kitchen floor. "Let's get . . . fired . . . up . . ."

Her voice trailed off at the sound of her dad's angry voice rising sharply. Holding her breath, Julie realized her parents were around the corner in the dining room. She debated if she should go on in, or sneak back outside.

When her dad spoke again, he sounded more tired than angry. "I never should have expanded my farming operation back when Julie was little. The two new sheds and corn bins seemed like a great idea at the time. Maybe if I hadn't done that, we'd be OK."

Sighing, his voice dropped to a whisper. "It's my fault we're in this mess."

Julie stood frozen in place, wishing she'd stayed outside.

"Roy, don't say that," Julie's mom pleaded. "You're not to blame. You couldn't have predicted the droughts these past two years. That's the cause of the problem—not you."

Julie jumped as her dad's fist pounded their round oak table. "I don't have control over *anything!* I can't control the prices I get for my crops, or the weather, or those infernal government programs!" Her dad's voice fell, and he spoke bitterly. "Why did I ever want to farm in the first place?"

Trapped in the stuffy kitchen, Julie wished she could escape. More and more often, her parents had been having these "discussions" at the dining room table.

Taking a deep breath, Julie reopened, then slammed the back door again. "I'm home!" she called out.

The voices in the dining room ceased. Buying time, Julie got a drink of water. She wrinkled her nose at the funny taste, dumped it down the sink, then forced herself to walk into the next room.

"How was school?" her mom asked. Although she smiled, the lines around her mouth deepened.

"Oh, the usual." Julie skipped over her news of the upcoming tryouts, feeling her enthusiasm would be out of place. She glanced at her dad, who stared out the window. "Hi, Dad."

Rubbing a roughened hand over his graying hair, her dad barely looked at her. "Hi, Honey." Pushing back his chair, he shuffled to the kitchen, where Julie soon heard the rattle of the antacid bottle.

"Is Dad OK?" Julie whispered. More and more these days, he reached for the antacids. *Rolaids* was scribbled on the grocery list almost every week.

"He'll be fine," her mom said, patting Julie's bare arm.

"But what's wrong with him? Nobody ever says." Without warning, her dad reappeared in the doorway. "I'm sick of being talked about behind my back!" he snapped. "If you have something to say, say it to my face!"

Julie gasped, then shrank back as if she'd been struck. Her hands made tight fists in her lap. "I—I—" Her fingernails dug into the palms of her hands.

"Roy! Julie's concerned about you."

The anger drained from her dad's face, and he rubbed his eyes. "I'm sorry, Honey." Roy McGregor leaned over to kiss the top of Julie's head. "I didn't mean to snarl at you."

"That's OK." Julie's chest felt as if it were being squeezed in a vise. She knew her dad loved her. Something terrible must be eating at him for him to act that way.

Julie's mom refilled their ceramic coffee mugs. "Julie has a point. We *haven't* told her very much."

"You know why," Mr. McGregor snapped. "It's my problem, and I'll handle it."

Julie stared at the yellow and orange gourd centerpiece, gathering courage to speak. "Dad, what exactly *is* wrong?"

"I said I don't want—" He spoke through clenched teeth. Then, rubbing the back of his sunburned neck, he started over. "The bank's riding me. It's going to be tough making the farm payment."

"Oh." Julie frowned. "When's it due?"

"December first."

Julie leaned forward. "That's good, isn't it? I mean, December's a long ways off, and you don't have all the crop out yet. Won't that pay off the bank loan?"

Her dad was shaking his head before she finished her question. "With droughts two years in a row, the crops are pitiful. And with the prices so low, it hardly pays to harvest."

"It's not *quite* that bad," Julie's mom interjected.

"Close enough," her dad argued, waving a callused hand. "I can't pay off the loan we already have, yet we'll probably need to borrow more soon to drill a new well."

Julie nodded, remembering the previous summer. With the well going dry for a while last June, they knew the water table was very low.

Her dad tasted his coffee, then pushed away his full cup. "It's going dry again. The coffee's lousy now that the drinking water tastes like metal again. The pressure's down lately too."

Julie had noticed the same thing, especially when she took a shower. There was hardly enough water pressure to rinse the shampoo out of her hair.

When their well had gone dry in June, they'd pulled up the eighty feet of pipe and attached another three-foot length, in order to reach down to where the water level had sunk. With the pressure dropping again, Julie knew time was running out. And this time they couldn't add more pipe—there was no more room down in the well.

"If the well goes dry again, then what?"

"We hope that won't happen." Her mom warmed her hands around her coffee cup. "If it does, we're too far from the rural water hookup, so that's out. We probably do have water down further, but we'd need someone to drill us a new, deeper well."

"Is that very expensive?" Julie tugged at the fringe on the tablecloth.

Her dad snorted. "Not if you have an extra seven or eight thousand dollars laying around."

"That much?" Julie's eyes opened wide. "So what do we do?"

Her dad shrugged and leaned back in his chair. *"That,* Julie, is the $64,000 question."

Julie's mom carried the cups to the kitchen, motioning for Julie to follow. Filling a small bowl with milk, she warmed it in the microwave, then headed outside.

"Let's sit in the swing as soon as I do something," she suggested.

Julie followed and watched her mom push the dish under the lilac bush by the corner of the house. Huge blue eyes stared out from a frightened gray face. "Another stray?" Julie asked, smiling.

Her mom nodded. “Here, kitty. Come here.” Straightening, she grinned sheepishly. “I know we don’t need any more cats, but this skinny one looked starved when it showed up this morning.”

Back on the porch, Julie nudged aside three cats to make room in the sun-warmed swing. The russet of the sugar maple leaves contrasted vividly with the clear blue sky. Squeals echoed from the hay rack near the barn, where Karen marched back and forth, twirling her battered silver baton.

Julie and her mother swung back and forth in silence, enjoying the immense quiet of the empty countryside.

Finally her mom spoke. “Dad didn’t mean to be so gruff just now. He’s got a lot on his mind.”

“And stomach,” Julie added, remembering the antacids.

“That too,” her mom agreed. “That concerns me.”

Tomma, their yellow and white tomcat, leaped into Julie’s lap, stretching and sinking his claws through her jeans. After prying his paws loose, Julie laid the cat on his back to rub his furry stomach. Soon he was purring.

“If Dad can’t make that bank payment, then what?”

“I imagine we would be forced to sell our last eighty acres. Since it’s been in your dad’s family for three generations, the idea of selling it hurts a lot.”

Julie gasped. Sell their last piece of land? What would they do then? She couldn’t imagine any other kind of life.

Even though her dad worked odd jobs in the winter,

farming was the only full-time occupation he'd ever known. Julie knew her dad would rather die than quit farming.

At one time they'd owned 320 acres. Julie's great-grandfather had homesteaded a piece of their farmland in the early 1900's, breaking the soil with a plow pulled by a team of horses. The farm had been turned over to the sons in the family who wanted to farm.

The cat's motorized purr grew louder. Julie absent-mindedly scratched behind his ears as she thought back.

Life had been good for her family until the year her little sister Karen was born. Julie wasn't sure what had happened exactly, but life had changed for her family then, as well as many of their neighbors.

"This is scary, isn't it?" Julie said, rubbing the goose bumps on her arm.

"In some ways, yes. I'm concerned about your dad's health, but I'm not worried about the rest of it. I *refuse* to worry about it."

Julie gripped the edge of the swing, getting a splinter in her palm. "How can you say that? I'm worried sick that we'll lose our farm!"

Julie's mom stared out across the yellow stubble cornfields, bathed in warm sunshine. "You're still young. By the time you're my age, you'll have weathered enough storms to know for sure that God is faithful—and that He keeps His promises."

"I know that," Julie protested, squeezing out the splinter. "But . . . does that really help at a time like this?"

"It's the *only* thing that helps at a time like this," her mom said. "God has promised to supply all our needs, and I believe Him. A place to live, a job for your dad, water—all those things are very real needs. God *will* supply. We have to do our part, and trust God to do His part."

With her finger, Julie made little swirls in Tomma's fur. She envied her mom's assurance. As for herself, her stomach hurt so bad that she was tempted to chew a couple of her dad's antacids.

"I wish I'd known earlier that we were in this much trouble," Julie finally said. "I want to help."

"I know you do."

"I mean it. Since money's so tight, I don't want any allowance anymore. I'll carry a sack lunch, too, instead of buying hot lunches." She made a mental note to get a refund for the rest of her lunch ticket.

"You don't need to do that."

"You said we needed to do our part." Julie watched the stray gray kitten lapping up milk. "I'm a member of this family too, and I want to help."

Her mom looked at her a long time, then smiled. "OK, if that's how you feel." She leaned over and kissed Julie's cheek. "When did you get so grown up?"

"Oh, Mom." Embarrassed, Julie pushed Tomma off her

lap, then stood. "I've got a ton of math homework. I think I'll get started."

"Good idea." As Julie started across the porch, her mom called after her, "Just remember what I said. Don't worry."

Julie nodded and slipped inside. She grabbed her book bag, then detoured through the living room and on upstairs.

In her room, she stopped at the card table set up in the corner. On it was her latest 1000-piece puzzle, a picture of a New England fishing village.

In a few minutes, she'd finished the peak of the sailing ship's mast, then added the flag flying at the top. Julie loved puzzles, and usually had one partially put together. She loved watching the pictures take shape as the tiny multicolored squares were connected, making sense out of all the unrelated pieces.

Julie glanced at her clock. It had only been forty minutes since she'd jumped off the bus, anxious to practice her cheerleading routines. Winning a place on the squad had been the only thing on her mind. Waves of guilt washed over Julie. How could she have been so wrapped up in herself, when their world was crumbling around them?

Julie stared at the wall, following the parade of rainbows across her wallpaper. Thinking back, she should have guessed something was seriously wrong: all her parents' hush-hush discussions that stopped when she entered the room, her dad's complaints about the new "upstart" banker in Elmwood, the disappearing bottles of Rolaids . . .

And Julie knew it wasn't just their family. She'd overheard plenty of talk about their neighbors' troubles. One family down the road had started buying groceries with food stamps. Some other farmers had had to sell part of their livestock or machinery to help pay off debts. In the past couple years, several families in their area had lost their entire farms.

Vaguely aware of noise outside, Julie sat up and peered out the dusty window. Below, her mother pushed four-year-old Karen on the tire swing, laughing and blowing kisses as Karen swept up and back, up and back. Shaking her head, Julie wondered how her mother could be so calm, even if she did believe God would meet all their needs.

Leaning her head against the smudged glass, she recalled her mom's last words outside in the swing. "Don't worry," she'd said.

*If only it were that easy!* Julie thought.

Grabbing her quilted pillow, she wrapped her arms around it. They were in danger of losing their farm—their whole way of life, really—and all her mother says is, "Don't worry." Oh, sure.

Talk about asking the impossible!

*Chapter 2*

# *Going Into Business*

After a restless night of disturbing dreams, Julie awoke with a quiet determination to help her family. Keeping one eye on the clock, she threw together a sack lunch while munching her cinnamon toast, pleased with the sacrifice she was making.

Outside the ground was covered with flaky white frost. Julie's breath escaped in billowy clouds as she waited for the bus. A few minutes later, it squealed to a stop and she climbed aboard. She slid onto the cracked, vinyl seat beside her neighbor, Monica Daniels.

"What's in the sack?" Monica asked, grabbing the bag. "Your material for home ec?"

"No, my lunch." Julie reclaimed her sack, then was pressed back into the seat as the bus lurched forward.

"What'd you bring your lunch for? Are we having something really gross today?" Monica pursed her red, glossy lips.

"I don't know. I just felt like bringing my lunch." Julie refused to tell Monica the real reason. Monica's big mouth would have the McGregors' money problems spread all over the school before first period. She tried to change the subject. "Are those new shoes?" she asked.

Refusing to be sidetracked, Monica peered through narrowed eyes and sniffed like a bloodhound. "*No*body in middle school carries a sack lunch. I mean, *really,* Julie. You're out of it enough without doing something this weird."

"Thanks a lot." Her mouth in a thin line, Julie stared out the window at the weeds in the ditch, yellowed by the first frost.

Monica wiped a dusty smudge from her new white tennis shoes. "Well, don't say I didn't warn you. If you want to be a social outcast, go ahead." Her voice was ominous. "Just remember—social outcasts don't become cheerleaders."

Julie glared at Monica, mentally strangling her. As if she didn't feel bad enough already!

Half an hour later, after transferring at Timmons Grove to another bus, Julie arrived at Laurel-Elmwood Middle School. Reluctantly, she heeded Monica's warning and tucked her lunch sack under her jacket. She'd stash it in her locker before anyone else asked nosy questions.

At lunch, Julie hid her sack in the folds of her skirt as she stood in the lunch line between Monica and Heather Sherman. The tantalizing aroma of spaghetti and garlic bread made her stomach growl. As they edged to the head of the line, Julie stepped aside self-consciously.

"Um, I'll save us a table," she mumbled.

Heather, her new friend from Laurel, felt Julie's forehead. "What's the matter? Are you sick?"

"No, I brought my lunch today." Embarrassed, Julie held out her crumpled brown sack.

"But spaghetti and coffee cake's your favorite!" Heather pushed her bushy red hair off her face.

Julie backed away, shrugging. "I'm not that hungry today."

Turning toward the lunch room, she claimed an empty table for them. Two boys snickered as they passed by with their plastic trays of steaming food. As mouth-watering as the spaghetti smelled, she'd lost her appetite.

Head down, Julie lectured herself sternly. *This isn't so bad. We aren't the only family with money problems. It's not a big deal.* She knew that at least ten kids in her class received reduced-priced lunches because they couldn't afford the full eighteen dollars for a lunch ticket.

A minute later the table was filled as Monica, Heather, Andrea Austin, and two other sixth graders jammed their trays together. Self-consciously, Julie opened her sack and removed her sandwich and Baggie of potato chips.

Piling a mound of parmesan cheese on her spaghetti, Andrea Austin pointed to Julie's peanut butter sandwich. "Didn't you get enough of that in grade school?"

"I *told* her only social misfits carry sack lunches," Monica piped up.

Fuming, Julie swallowed the tasteless lump of bread. "I just wanted to carry my lunch. Is that OK with *you?"* she snapped.

"OK, OK. Don't bite my head off!"

Julie sighed. "Sorry."

After a moment of awkward silence, Monica switched topics to the upcoming cheerleading tryouts. At least a dozen girls were trying out for the six positions on the squad, and Julie knew the competition would be stiff.

She stared at her half-eaten sandwich. Could Monica be right about this making her a social outcast and hurting her chances at the tryouts? Julie shook her head. Surely not. It couldn't be *that* important. Most likely, it was just one more of Monica's dramatic lines.

Just then Mike Bloom, a boy from Julie's homeroom, waltzed by with his empty tray. "Hey, McGregor, where'd you get the sack lunch? Ripping off poor, defenseless kindergartners these days?" Snorting, he swaggered off.

Monica leaned over, her star-shaped earrings bobbing. "I *told* you what would happen," she said, whispering loud enough for the whole table to hear. "Just listen to me—"

Julie shoved her chair back and stuffed the remainder of

her lunch in the paper sack. Twelve minutes remained in the lunch period, and she couldn't sit through any more insults. "I'm going outside," she said.

Tossing her sack in the dented garbage can by the door, Julie hurried outside to a spot under the low-hanging branches of a red-orange maple tree. Leaning against the trunk, she closed her eyes and breathed deeply several times.

Gradually her face cooled off, leaving her feeling rather silly. Why had she let Monica get under her skin?

"Julie, are you all right?"

Startled, Julie opened her eyes and stood up straight. The principal, Mrs. Oswald, towered over her. At least six feet tall, the principal added another five inches to her height with an elaborate beehive hairdo. Julie suspected that her height was meant to intimidate the students. If so, it worked.

"Um, I'm just fine, Mrs. Oswald," Julie stammered.

"Then why aren't you inside eating lunch with the others?"

"I already ate. I mean, I didn't really eat, but I brought my lunch." At Mrs. Oswald's puzzled frown, Julie stumbled on. "I wasn't hungry after all," she ended lamely.

"But you're not sick?" The tall woman laced her fingers together behind her back, then paced back and forth in front of Julie. Abruptly, she stopped and turned. "Would you like to tell me what the problem is?"

Julie stared at the dry ground, scuffing her tennis shoe back and forth through the leaves. Her dad said they should keep their problems to themselves, and she agreed with him.

"Julie?" the principal prodded.

Wishing Mrs. Oswald would go away, Julie lifted her chin stubbornly. "We're having some money problems at home. I'm helping cut expenses by carrying my lunch. That's all."

Mrs. Oswald nodded. "So many farm families are experiencing the same thing." She brushed some lint from her tweed skirt. "I'd be happy to check into reduced-priced lunches for you."

Julie's face flamed in embarrassment. "No, thank you," she said stiffly. "My dad would never allow that. We don't want charity." She'd heard him say over and over that they didn't take "handouts." Anyway, even with the price reduced, the lunches would still cost money.

"It isn't charity," Mrs. Oswald explained. "We're just lending a helping hand."

"I can't," Julie repeated, "but thank you, just the same."

The principal paced back and forth again. Other kids, now finished with their lunches, wandered outside for the last few minutes of their break. From across the yard, a giggling group of seventh-grade girls pointed at Julie and Mrs. Oswald.

The principal stopped, clicking the heels of her black

shoes together. "I appreciate your not wanting 'charity,' as you call it. What about this instead?"

She rolled back and forth on the balls of her feet, her beehive brushing the curled leaves on the lowest branch. Julie eyed her warily, wishing she'd keep her booming voice lower. "You need to eat. I could arrange for a job, having you work in the cafeteria in return for free lunches. You'd be *earning* your lunches that way. We'd have to rearrange your schedule a bit, but it could be done, I'm sure."

A job? Julie chewed her lip thoughtfully, recalling her mom's words the night before. Maybe this was one way God intended to supply their needs. From the corner of her eye, Julie saw Heather approaching.

"Um, can I think about it for a while?" she whispered.

"Sure. Just let me know." Turning, Mrs. Oswald strode briskly up the cracked sidewalk to the double front doors.

Brushing cat hair from her sweater, Heather cleared her throat. "I didn't mean to eavesdrop, but I heard what Mrs. Oswald said." She laid a hand on Julie's arm. "I'm sorry your family's having trouble, but I think a job in the cafeteria might be fun."

Julie stared at her in disbelief. *"Fun?"*

"Sure." Heather linked her arm through Julie's when the buzzer rang. They trudged up the hill together. "Having a real job would be neat. You could look at it as—as an adventure."

Rolling her eyes, Julie smiled halfheartedly, grateful for

her friend's support. She did appreciate it, but no amount of encouragement would turn this embarrassing situation into an adventure.

By the end of the week, Julie still hadn't mentioned Mrs. Oswald's job offer at home, but it was starting to appeal to her. Julie had carried her lunch all week, but instead of dying down, the ridicule had increased every day. The last two days she'd even saved her lunch to eat after school on the bus. Although she was starving by then, she only had Monica's jeers to endure.

Plodding down the bus steps Friday afternoon, Julie looked forward to the weekend more than usual. For the next two days she didn't have to carry her lunch in a bag—or be laughed at while she ate it.

In the front yard, Karen squealed and waved as she tore across the lawn and catapulted into a pile of leaves. Thrashing wildly, she kicked curled maple leaves in all directions. Then, scooping them back into a haphazard pile, she ran to Julie. Hanging on her arm, she swung back and forth.

"Come jump in the leaves with me," Karen begged. *"Please?"*

Julie laughed, glad to see that *Karen's* spirits, at least, weren't affected by the gloom and doom in the house. "Let me change clothes first." Julie pried Karen loose and flexed her arm. "Then I'll come back out. You could practice your twirling while I practice my cheers."

"That's even better!" Karen threw leaves over her head to rain down around her. Then, turning a lopsided cartwheel, she landed squarely on her blue-jeaned bottom.

Laughing, Julie headed inside and set her book bag on the kitchen counter. "Hi, Dad," she said to his back.

"Hi, Honey." He emerged from the refrigerator and poured a large glass of 2% milk. "How was school?"

"OK. I got a B+ on my geology test."

Mr. McGregor smiled. "That's good." His smile faded into deep lines around his mouth.

Julie studied her dad as he sipped his milk. Why was he dressed in church clothes, complete with a tie? And why was he inside the house on a beautiful fall day, instead of out picking corn? Had he been to a funeral or something?

"Did you go anywhere special?" she asked. "I just wondered, since you're all dressed up."

He drained his glass and set it in the sink. "I've been to the bank. I gave my projection for the coming year to that new young banker, Mr. Curtis."

"What did he say?"

"Not much. I tried to convince him to give me more time on the loan, but this new banker isn't too sympathetic." He laughed harshly, and the sound grated on Julie's ears. "I wish Ed still ran the bank. He understood us farmers and knew what we were up against. Mr. Curtis just keeps referring to the 'bottom line.'"

Julie's dad reached for the plastic antacid bottle. The milk hadn't helped his sore stomach much, Julie thought.

"If the extension gets turned down, what will you do?"

"Good question." He chewed the chalky white tablets. "Guess I'll be like everyone else and get another job. I do know something about mechanics, so maybe something along that line. I just don't know." Shoulders slumped, he shuffled out of the room, then turned. "I need to get back in the field. Your mom's at the grocery store. When she gets home, tell her I'll be real late tonight. The forecast is for rain tomorrow."

Julie nodded silently as her dad disappeared upstairs. She tried to imagine her dad working as a mechanic instead of farming. Doing odd jobs to fill time in the winter was one thing. Losing his independence by working full-time for someone else was different. Julie wondered if her dad could make the change.

Twenty minutes later, Julie was outside practicing her cheers when their dusty, brown station wagon pulled into the driveway.

"Come on, Karen." Julie cartwheeled to the house. Together, Julie, Karen, and their mom carried in the six heavy bags of groceries, then Karen raced back outside.

Sorting through the brown sacks, Julie separated the toothpaste, shampoo, and hand soap and took it to the bathroom. Back in the kitchen, she was arranging the canned fruit on the bottom shelf when she remembered.

"Dad said it's supposed to rain tomorrow, so he's going to work late."

"I'm not surprised. I'll take something out to the field later." Her mom paused, arms loaded down with milk and eggs. "How did he seem to you, Julie?"

"Depressed." Closing the cupboard door, Julie's knees cracked as she straightened up. "He talked about finding another job if the loan extension is turned down."

Julie's mom nodded as she folded sacks. "He's worried about finding enough work to support us." She put away the oranges, lettuce, and cheese, then turned to Julie. Her eyes sparkled. *"However,* I think I might have an answer. At least a temporary one."

"Really? What is it?"

"In the checkout line I read the stuff on the bulletin board, the one where people advertise for things." Julie's mom clapped her hands together. "I saw an ad for a day care center, and it gave me an idea for a job."

"You want to go to work at a day care center in New Hampton?"

"No, something better. I was thinking of opening my *own* day care center, right here." She threw her arms wide. "What do you think of that?"

"Um, let me think." Julie thought of several objections, but she hated to throw cold water on her mom's idea. It had been weeks since she'd looked this happy.

"This is what I had in mind," her mom continued as she

cut up a roasting chicken. "So many mothers have gone back to work, and good day care is hard to find. If I were a working mom, I'd love to have my kids spend their days in the country, at a place like ours."

"That's true. We have lots of room to play outside."

"And by working at home, I'd be here with Karen. Frankly, we need the money, and if I ran a day care center, I wouldn't have to work in town and leave Karen with a baby-sitter."

"The idea *does* have possibilities," Julie admitted. "But how will you get the kids to come? What if you can't find enough kids to make the idea pay? What about a day care license—do you need one? What if kids get sick?"

"Whoa, whoa!" Her mom waved a chicken leg at her. "If the Lord approves of the plan, He'll work it out. Let's take one day at a time. There's enough to worry about today without worrying about tomorrow too." She tossed the chicken in a plastic bag of seasonings and shook it briskly.

"Sorry." Julie smiled sheepishly. "So, what can I do to help?"

Her mom put the coated chicken in the oven, then dried her hands on a towel. "I *just* happen to have a few ideas."

For the next half hour, they sat hunched over at the table making "To Do" lists—one for Julie, one for her mom. Julie's mom would find out about registering her home for day care, get an ad into the *Elmwood Times,* and draw up some menus and schedules. Julie's jobs included making posters to advertise the new baby-sitting service and putting them up in town.

Julie worked hard all weekend, then put her eight posters up in Elmwood after school on Monday. By the end of that week, after the phone rang steadily every evening, her mom had lined up twelve children, including two babies. Most of the kids would be there all day, but four would arrive on the school bus after school and stay till suppertime. Julie was almost as excited as her mom when each new name was added to the list on the cork bulletin board.

The only thing that dampened her enthusiasm was her dad's reaction to the baby-sitting plan. Although he'd officially given his OK, Julie watched him as he withdrew day by day, growing quieter and more thoughtful.

By the end of the week, it was as if he'd gone into a room, locked the door, and thrown away the key.

*Chapter 3*

# *Embarrassment*

"Is this the place?" Julie asked as they pulled into a parallel parking place on New Hampton's Main Street. "I'd never heard of it before."

"Me, neither," her mom replied, "until Marge at church told me about it. She gets all her kids' clothes here."

Forcing a smile, Julie sank lower into the seat. If she hadn't outgrown her jeans and blouses to an embarrassing degree, she would never have considered shopping here. The store appeared presentable enough, even inviting, the way its name was splashed across the plate glass in neon-red letters. But dazzling or not, "The Fashion Exchange" was still a consignment shop.

Julie hid her face behind her long hair. She couldn't believe that they'd been reduced to buying *used* clothes.

As she climbed out of the car, Julie scanned the crowded sidewalk for people she knew. Even though New Hampton was twenty miles from home, all her friends shopped there, since Elmwood had nothing but the grain co-op and a "Kum 'N Go" convenience store.

Her mom locked the car doors, then took Karen's hand. "Thank goodness there are stores like this," she said brightly. "With the economy down, I guess they're springing up all over. There are two others in town if we don't find anything here."

"Um, great." Julie tried to sound enthusiastic, but failed.

Although she was glad her mom had found an affordable clothing store, to Julie it seemed like buying her school clothes at some tacky garage sale. However, no matter how much she hated wearing other people's castoffs, she *wouldn't* complain, she reminded herself. Wearing used jeans was a small thing compared to her parents' worries.

"Oooh, Mommy, look!" Karen pointed to the front window, where a child-sized mannequin wore a fuzzy sweater appliqued with pink rabbits. "It's just my size! Can we buy that?"

"I'd love to, Honey, but not today." Mrs. McGregor held the door while the girls slipped inside. "Today we're buying clothes for Julie."

Julie braced herself, but once inside, she blinked in surprise. The store was brightly lit and roomy, with overhead ceiling fans, instead of the dingy, cramped quarters she'd expected. Long racks of men's, women's, and children's clothes, marked with different colored tags, stretched to the back of the store. At the front, near the cash register, was a display of ties, belts, jewelry, mittens, scarves, and purses.

"There's a bigger selection than I expected," Julie admitted, standing on tiptoe. At the back of the store, near the dressing rooms, she spotted a long rack of wedding gowns, veils, and bridesmaid dresses. They looked like brand new.

"Oh, Julie, look at this." Her mom held up a lavender sweater interwoven with shiny, metallic threads. "It isn't worn at all, but the price tag says only five dollars."

Julie moved to the size five section of the jeans rack. Cleaned and pressed, they hung in neat rows. Her hopes rose as she thumbed through the jeans. They looked almost new, and the average price was only a third of the department stores'.

"May I help you?"

Julie jumped. A young salesgirl stood behind her. "I'm just looking, thanks. I'm surprised how nice the clothes are."

The young girl laughed. "People are often amazed the first time they come in. They expect flea market quality." She pointed to a curtained doorway near the back. "My boss is back there now with someone who dropped off some clothes. The owner only keeps the nicest ones to resell."

Nodding, Julie picked out three pairs of jeans to try on. "I'll be right back," she called to her mom.

At the dressing area, she slipped into a tiny cubicle and pulled the curtain closed, sliding it on its large wooden rings. Inside was a long mirror, several hooks, and a vinyl chair.

Julie was zipping up the first pair of jeans when Karen dove under the curtain, yanking it partly open. "Karen, get out of here!" Julie yanked the curtain closed again. "I want some privacy."

"But guess what!"

"I don't want to 'guess what.' Now scram."

Reluctantly Karen dropped to all fours and crawled out under the curtain. Ten minutes later, Julie had also finished trying on the pink jeans and the faded denims. The pink pair was too tight, but the other two pair fit perfectly. Jeans draped over her arm, Julie pulled aside the curtain and stepped out.

At the front of the store, standing by the cash register, were Monica Daniels and her mother.

Julie stepped back in the dressing room to hide. Monica was the last person she'd wanted to run into. And yet . . .

Peeking around the curtain, Julie watched Monica try on several leather belts while her mother talked with Julie's mom. If Monica, with all her money and fashion know-how, didn't mind shopping at The Fashion Exchange, then Julie decided it must be OK. After seeing the prices here, it explained why Monica had so many clothes.

Just then, Monica turned. Spying Julie, she waved a belt in the air. "Hey, get a load of this!" Tying a gold-spangled sash around her middle, Monica danced in the aisle, making the golden tassels fly.

Julie laughed. "Are you going to buy it?"

"Maybe. I love trying on this junk, don't you?" Monica tossed it back on the rack. "Hey. Let's look at the wedding gowns."

Hesitating, Julie glanced over her shoulder. Near the winter coats, her mom chatted with Mrs. Daniels. Karen marched up and down the aisles, wearing three striped scarves, red mittens, and a hat; a pink price tag dangled between her eyes.

Leaving the jeans on the counter, Julie followed Monica to the bridal gown section, where Monica tried on three pearl-covered, wispy white veils.

Mrs. Daniels then called to her daughter. "Let's go, Monica. I have to get to work."

Dropping the veil on the floor, Monica sauntered over to the two mothers. Sighing, Julie carefully hung up the delicate headpiece, then followed.

"Hello, Julie." Mrs. Daniels rolled her heavily made-up eyes. "Do you enjoy looking at the wedding gowns too?"

Julie shrugged. "They're OK, I guess."

Mrs. Daniels shook her head teasingly. "You can't fool me. It won't be long before you're looking at wedding gowns for *real!"* She turned to Julie's mom. "Our girls are growing up fast. Monica's taller than I am already."

Linda McGregor put her arm around Julie. "I hate to even think about that yet."

Indignant, Monica jutted out her hip. "When *I* get married, I'm not buying *my* wedding dress here. Only bums and hobos wear used clothes." Nose turned up, she sniffed the air as if detecting something offensive.

Julie heard a gasp, but when she glanced up, her mom's lips were pressed tightly together.

*That's a dumb remark for Monica to make,* Julie thought angrily, *since she shops here herself!*

Julie's mom broke the awkward silence. "How did the jeans fit, Julie?"

"Two pair fit great. I left them over there on the counter."

"You're *buying* clothes here?" Monica burst out. "You wear *used* clothes?" Several customers in the store turned at her shrill voice.

"Monica, hush." Mrs. Daniels paled, then blushed, leaving two red blotches of color on her cheeks. "I'm sorry, Linda."

Her mom remained silent, but Julie wanted to clobber Monica. "What a lot of nerve." Julie jabbed a finger at Monica. *"You're* shopping here, so what's the big deal?"

Monica's mouth hung open for a moment, then she simply hooted. Holding her sides, she howled with laughter until her eyes brimmed with tears.

"You thought I came here to *buy* clothes? I don't believe it." She wiped her running eyes on her sweater sleeve. "I'm here with Mom to leave some outgrown clothes to sell. This is where I bring clothes I don't want anymore." Head thrown back, she dissolved into bubbling laughter again. "You actually thought I was here to buy clothes!"

"Monica!" Mrs. Daniels shook her daughter's arm. "That's enough." Nervously licking her coral lips, she glanced first at Julie, then Julie's mom. She groped for the right words. "I just assumed you were here to leave clothes or collect money. I had no idea . . . What I mean is . . ."

Mrs. McGregor's faced turned four shades of red, and her dark eyes snapped. "It's a natural mistake," she said quietly. "We arrived while you were in the back room. Julie needs some clothes."

"Oh, please let us help," Mrs. Daniels interrupted, her silver earrings swinging. "I'll go in the back and get Monica's clothes before the owner tags them. Monica's a size or two bigger than Julie. The clothes we brought in today should fit Julie just right."

"No, thank you. That's very kind, but no."

"I don't mind, honestly." Mrs. Daniels laid her hand on

Linda McGregor's arm. Her long fingernails were painted maroon, and several rings glittered on her fingers. "What are neighbors for, if they can't help out?"

Julie wished she could drop through the floor before she died of shame. Holding her breath, Julie watched her mom's expression change from embarrassment to anger to uncertainty, then back to embarrassment.

"I appreciate the offer, but no, thank you." Julie's mom squared her shoulders. "We can pay for the clothes."

"Well, if you're sure . . ." Mrs. Daniels' voice trailed off as they backed away.

Julie stared at the polished, black-and-white tiled floor. Finally, the tiny gold bell over the front door jingled, and she knew that Monica and her mom were gone. Glancing up, she headed to the blouse section, pretending not to see her mother's embarrassment.

Thumbing through white cotton shirts, flowered silk blouses, and lace-trimmed tops, Julie considered her mother's reaction. Julie knew that having to carry sack lunches and buy secondhand clothes embarrassed *her*. However, Julie had never imagined that these necessities hurt her mother too.

The next week swept by. A whirlwind of activity kept Julie too busy to worry much about wearing secondhand clothes. Between going to school, doing her homework, practicing her flute and cheerleading routines, keeping a watchful eye on her dejected dad, and helping with the day care kids after school, she dropped into bed exhausted every night.

And she wasn't the only one, Julie knew. Since six kids arrived at 7 a.m. for breakfast, Julie's mom was up every morning by five. First she flew through her housework and got the farm bookkeeping up to date, then laid out the Cheerios and bananas for the first arrivals. Two more kids arrived before eight o'clock. So, except for blowing a kiss when Julie dashed out the door, her mom barely noticed her. After school, four more elementary kids would come home with Julie.

By the beginning of the second week, her mom had established a routine at their Country Care Center. Meals, snacks, naps, and playtimes were scheduled. Julie watched as her mom flew from task to task, usually with a drooling baby in her arms. It wasn't much fun, but Julie didn't mind pitching in after school when she saw how hard her mom was working.

One thing she *did* mind very much, however. That was the lack of privacy.

On Tuesday that week, she arrived home to find four-year-old Meghan jumping on her bed trampoline-style, dressed in Julie's best fleecy bathrobe. Two of her dresser drawers had been pulled out and the contents dumped on the floor.

On Thursday afternoon, Julie found the three-year-old twin girls shaking her favorite bath talc around the room.

Coughing and choking through the billowing cloud of powder, Julie retrieved the nearly empty container. She opened a window, hoping that the dusty haze would be sucked outside. That night it took Julie an hour to vacuum and dust her room.

But Friday afternoon was the worst. Racing up the stairs, Julie flung open her bedroom door and was nearly knocked flat by an overpowering odor. Sitting in the middle of her bed, surrounded by a large wet circle, sat three-year-old Devin. He took one look at Julie and burst into hysterical sobs.

"Bad boy!" he wailed. "Devin all wet. Bad boy!"

Groaning, Julie dropped her books on her desk. "Bad boy is right," she muttered, holding her nose.

Unless she was much mistaken, he was more than wet. She rolled her eyes, searching for a way to remove the smelly toddler without actually touching him. With her mom busy downstairs with eleven other kids, Julie couldn't call for help. Sighing, she tried not to gag as she approached the bed.

"Stop crying, Devin. It'll be all right."

She leaned over, opened the window, and breathed deeply. The cold air stung. After several gulps of fresh air, Julie hooked her hands under Devin's armpits, a place that would surely be safe, she reasoned.

"Don't spank bad boy!" Devin wailed, thrashing about.

"I won't! Now hold still." Julie winced at the mess on

her bed, but knew she'd have to clean that up later. First things first. She had to get this stinky kid downstairs. "Come on, kiddo. Let me show you what the potty chair's for."

With outstretched arms, Julie carried Devin to the bathroom. "Now stay put." She pointed a warning finger at him. "I have to get your diaper bag."

In the dining room, she found the blue plaid bag marked "Devin." Behind her at the table, her mom was pouring the second round of Kool-Aid for the school kids' afternoon snack. With a wiggly toddler balanced on her hip, she moved from glass to glass as kids cried, "More! More!"

Her mom turned around when the plastic pitcher ran dry. "What are you looking for?" she asked.

Julie dug to the bottom of the bag and tried to sound calm. "More training pants for Devin."

"Oh, no." Julie's mom rolled her eyes. "That's about the tenth time today. I don't see why his mother doesn't leave him here in diapers."

"Isn't there some way you can keep these kids downstairs and out of my bedroom?" Julie asked. "He wet on my bed this time, and now I have to change my bedding. I already had a ton of homework to do."

Julie's mom snatched the training pants out of Julie's hand. "I'm sorry," she snapped. "I ordered one of those collapsible gates to put at the bottom of the stairs. It hasn't arrived yet." Stomping out of the room, she called over her shoulder, "Go do your homework then. *I'm* not busy. *I* never get tired, so I don't need your help."

Hurt by her sharp tone, Julie tried to convince herself that her mom didn't mean what she'd said. She was exhausted. Keeping track of twelve kids would drive anybody nuts.

"Look out!" one of the kids at the table screamed.

Julie jumped up in time to stop the flow of Kool-Aid from dribbling onto the carpet. With half a dozen paper towels, she mopped up the mess, then sent the kids out to play. Thank goodness it was a sunny day, Julie thought. What would they do when it got too cold for the kids to play outside?

Julie shook her head as she wiped the sticky table. What had gone wrong? Two weeks ago the Country Care Center had sounded like the answer to their prayers. Now it seemed more like a nightmare. They'd always loved the peace and quiet of the country, the leisurely family times together. Overnight, it had been replaced by screaming chaos.

From the dining room window, Julie watched half a dozen children race across the gravel driveway, churning up dust. Their piercing screeches filled the air.

Whether they were able to keep the farm or not, Julie wondered if things would ever be the same again.

*Chapter 4*

# *Tryouts*

The weekend was blissfully quiet without the dozen day care children. After vacuuming and folding laundry, Julie spent Saturday afternoon practicing her cheerleading routines for the tryouts on Monday. She'd learned all six cheers, but she wouldn't know until the tryouts which two cheers she'd be required to perform.

That night she dropped into bed, satisfied that she was ready. The next day, she'd run through the cheers again, then rest up. Sundays were always relaxing days.

However, Sunday morning started off on the wrong foot, then went from bad to worse. With one eye on the clock, Julie slipped on her shoes, grabbed her Bible, and headed outside. She hated being the last one out the door on the way to church, knowing the whole family was waiting for her in the car. However, that morning her mom and Karen were alone, and her mom sat behind the wheel.

"Where's Dad?" Julie asked, sliding into the front seat.

Her mom's voice was soft, but her lips were pressed into a thin line. "He isn't coming with us this morning."

Julie's heart sank, but she buckled on her seat belt in silence. Backing out of the driveway, she scanned the yard for her dad, but he was nowhere in sight.

In the back seat, Karen was soon singing at the top of her voice. Julie leaned close to her mom and whispered, "What's going on? Dad never misses church, not even to work in the field."

Mrs. McGregor passed a slow-moving tractor on the highway before answering. "I'm afraid he got some bad news yesterday. He doesn't feel like facing people yet."

"What news?"

"His request for an extension on the bank loan was turned down."

Julie counted the leaning fence posts they passed. "What exactly does that mean?" she finally asked.

Mrs. McGregor adjusted the rear view mirror, leaving a thumbprint on it. "To make a long story short, it means we have to sell our last eighty acres to pay off the bank loan."

Julie gasped. The last eighty acres! No wonder her dad was depressed. Then a somewhat comforting thought occurred to her. "Maybe no one will buy it. Hardly any farmers around here can afford to buy more land."

"That's true, but unfortunately that isn't what's happening to all the farmland. Lately some big corporation out east has bought up the farmland in our area, so it might not take too long to find a buyer." Her mom massaged her forehead, rubbing in tiny circles. "Your dad won't tell anyone he's having problems. It's a strain to pretend at church that everything's just fine."

"Why won't he tell anyone? We aren't the only farmers with money problems."

"For some reason, he thinks that talking about his problems is unmanly. And my day care business bothers him more than he's saying. Sometimes, when farmers can't support their wives and families, even for awhile, they don't feel like men anymore."

"That's not true!"

*"I* know that, and *you* know that, but men in your dad's family have been the sole support for generations. This makes him feel like a failure." Her hands tightened on the steering wheel. "I don't want my baby-sitting to make him feel bad, but we need the money. He knows that."

Julie nodded, aching inside for her dad's feelings of failure as well as her mother's worry and exhaustion. She knew they were both doing the best they could. At least her mom could talk with her friends at church that morning. Maybe she'd feel more optimistic on the way home.

Instead, the ride home was worse. When Julie climbed into the car with Karen, she noticed that her mom had gripped the steering wheel until her knuckles were white.

"What's wrong?" she asked, her heart pounding.

Mrs. McGregor shook her head in warning, nodded at Karen, then maneuvered out of the crowded parking lot. They were halfway home before Karen toppled over, asleep in the back seat.

Finally her mom spoke. "You know my friend, Ruth Jackson? Her husband farms in the next county." She caught a shaking breath. "He was notified this week that he was losing his farm. The bank foreclosed on them." Julie's mom grabbed a Kleenex from her purse. "He had a heart attack last night. He's still in intensive care at the hospital."

"Oh, Mom." Ignoring the rules, Julie unbuckled her seat belt and slid over. She patted her mom's arm, but felt helpless. "Are you worried that something like that will happen to Dad?"

"I don't know. It could. The stress just builds and builds." She chewed her lower lip. "If only he'd talk to someone! He won't talk to the minister or any of his friends, and now he doesn't want to talk to me either." Julie's mom breathed deeply several times. "I'm sorry. I didn't mean to burden you with this."

"It's OK." Julie put an arm around her mom's narrow shoulders. She'd never felt so helpless in her life.

During an awkward dinner, they pretended nothing was wrong, but Julie felt the threat in the air. Even Karen was

restrained, eating quietly, without her usual nonstop chatter about Sunday school.

That afternoon, Julie curled up on the living room couch to study for her math test, but she couldn't settle down and concentrate. The house was filled with an eerie stillness. Julie and her mom were both watching Julie's dad, but trying not to look like it. In the pit of her stomach, Julie sensed something horrible might happen, as if her dad were a ticking time bomb.

Needing a break, Julie wandered into the kitchen for a snack. She passed her dad's sturdy desk in the corner of the dining room, glanced down, and stopped short.

Scotch taped to the telephone was a number for the Farm Crisis Hotline. Julie stared till the bright red numbers blurred. Her mom must have taped the phone number there the minute they returned from church.

In the kitchen Julie ate three oatmeal cookies, but barely tasted them. After another half hour of fruitless studying, she quit and dropped her book on the floor. It was difficult to take a math test seriously when her whole life was unraveling.

The next morning on the bus, she tried again to study. But between Monica's long-winded jabbering beside her and the screaming kindergartners behind her, Julie couldn't concentrate there either. She gave up and watched the sunlit countryside roll by on the way to school.

Feeling doomed, she entered her first period math

class. An hour later, she emerged defeated. She knew without seeing the results that she'd just flunked her very first test.

At lunchtime, Julie was too nervous to eat the sandwich she'd brought, so she escaped outside to practice her cheers one last time. During fifth period, any girl trying out would be dismissed from classes to go to the gym. There, the principal and three teachers would watch and grade the routines. She'd heard that Miss Goodman, the band teacher, would be one of the judges. That helped a little.

Sitting on the hard bleachers next to Heather an hour later, Julie shivered as she watched the tryouts. Wiping her damp palms on her gym shorts, she tried to stop her knees from shaking. Her legs were itchy, dry and very white, Julie noticed with embarrassment. If only she still had a bit of her summer tan left.

In front of the bleachers, Monica finished her second cheer, which she did with real ease and grace, Julie thought enviously. *It must be nice to be coached by an older sister who's a cheerleader,* she thought.

Mrs. Oswald thanked Monica, then stood up, clipboard in hand. "Julie McGregor is next."

Heather squeezed Julie's arm. "Good luck."

"Thanks." Julie adjusted her ponytail, then walked to the center of the gym floor, in front of the judges. She forced herself to smile, but her stiff lips felt frozen. She was vaguely aware of Miss Goodman's encouraging smile.

"For your first cheer, we'd like you to do 'Victory,'" Mrs. Oswald boomed, pencil poised above her clipboard.

Julie let out the breath she'd been holding. This was one of her favorites; she'd practiced it dozens of times. Clearing her throat, she rested her hands on her hips, then nodded. The other girls chanted the cheer along with her.

"V! I-C! T-O! R-Y!" Julie shot her arms overhead. "Split that V! Dot that I! Curve that C-T-O-R-Y!" She waved her arms in descending spirals, then repeated the cheer.

At the end, a smattering of applause was followed by dead silence as the judges bent over their score sheets. Chewing on her lower lip, Julie waited.

"That was lovely, Julie," the principal said. "Next, we'd like you to do 'Let's Start.'"

Julie threw a panicky glance at Heather. This cheer often confused her at the end, with its complicated arm movements. Heather gave her a thumbs-up signal and grinned.

Again, Julie took her opening stance, this time with her arms straight overhead. Nodding, she began. "Are you ready to get started? Yes, we are!" she shouted, turning and twisting her arms in rhythm. "Are you ready to get started? Yes, we are! S, S-T, S-T-A-R-T, Let's start! S, S-T, S-T-A-R-T, Let's start!"

She ended in a split kick, one hand at her hip, one arm straight up. The applause was enthusiastic this time.

Wiping the perspiration that dripped down the sides of her face, Julie collapsed on her bleacher seat.

Heather grinned. "It's in the bag," she whispered.

"I wish!" Julie rolled her eyes, but she *did* appreciate Heather's support, especially since Heather was nervous herself about trying out. Julie turned her attention to the remaining performances.

That afternoon Julie scarcely heard a word during her classes as she waited for the intercom announcement. The overhead speaker crackled to life ten minutes before the final bell. Julie stared at her hands clasped tightly in her lap. Mrs. Oswald's voice was crisp as she announced the six new basketball cheerleaders.

Head down, Julie waited. She was aware of hearing both Monica's and Heather's names, but it wasn't until the sixth and final name was read that she heard her own—"Julie McGregor." She closed her eyes for a moment, whispered, "Thank You, Lord," then turned to accept the congratulations of the kids in her class.

After school, Julie couldn't wait to tell her mom she'd been chosen. Both Karen and her mom would be thrilled for her. After the bad news at church the day before, Julie hadn't even mentioned that the tryouts were that afternoon. She was grateful to bring home some *good* news for a change.

Stepping off the bus at four o'clock, Julie dodged the four extra day care kids. Oak trees arched overhead as she raced down her long driveway. Her hair streamed out behind her, and the late October sunshine warmed her face.

In the kitchen, Julie called out, “Mom? I’m home! Guess what?” She hurried into the dining room. A crowd of kids stood at the table, gulping orange Kool-Aid and coloring paper jack-o’-lanterns. “Bobby, where’s my mom?” she asked the red-headed four-year-old.

“Wook outside.” He pointed a stubby finger. “Winda’s helping Becky. She feww off a wadder in the barn.”

“Oh, no,” Julie muttered, running back outside. The kids were strictly forbidden to climb that rickety ladder to the hayloft. She just hoped Becky hadn’t broken a leg.

Curious kids blocked the barn doorway, and Julie pushed her way through. There, on the straw-covered cement floor, her mom knelt over Becky, examining her scraped legs.

Julie’s mom glanced up in relief. “I’m glad you’re home. We’ve had a little accident here.”

“Anything broken?” Julie knelt beside Becky, who sobbed quietly. Her tears mixed with the dirt on her face to form tiny rivulets of mud.

“I don’t think so, but I’ll go call the doctor just in case.” She stood and brushed the straw off her jeans. “If you’ll keep Becky calm, I’ll be right back.” Jumping over three cats, she dashed out the door.

“Oh, Mom, guess what!” Julie called, but her mom was already running toward the house.

Shrugging, Julie stayed beside Becky and held her dirty, trembling hand. She'd wait until after all the day care kids went home, *then* she'd tell her mom about the tryouts. For something this important, Julie felt she deserved her mom's undivided attention.

The next two hours passed in a blur. Dr. Reynolds arrived, assured them Becky was just bruised, then left. After locking the barn door, Julie's mom carried Becky inside, where she washed her up and applied Band-aids and disinfectant. Then, by the time Julie and her mom changed and fed the babies, it was time for parents to begin arriving.

At six o'clock, while her mom rocked a crying baby, Karen set the table. Julie fixed a meat loaf, scrubbed four potatoes, then put them in the microwave to bake. She had no idea when her dad would be in from the field, but it'd be super if she could make her announcement to everyone after sharing a relaxed meal together.

Julie sighed. It'd be just like old times.

However, half an hour later, her dad called on the radio to say that the elevator on the picker was jammed. He had to work through the supper hour to fix it.

"Base clear," Julie's mom said, clicking off the radio. Leaning against the counter, she closed her eyes a moment. "Since the day care kids are gone, I'll run Dad's supper out to the field. I'll take mine too." Sighing, she packed their hot food into covered plastic containers. "Could you give Karen a bath while I'm gone?"

"Sure." So much for her big announcement at supper. "Can I talk to you a minute when you get back?"

Her mom glanced up as she filled a dish with milk. "Are you OK?"

Julie nodded. "I just want to talk to you."

"You bet." Mrs. McGregor kissed both girls, then pushed open the door, juggling the sack of food and bowl of milk. "I'll give Charcoal the milk on my way."

"Charcoal? You mean the gray kitten?" Julie held the door for her mom and smiled. "You're such a soft touch."

"You're just as bad as I am!" she retorted. "See you later. We'll have a good visit the minute I get back."

Julie and Karen ate their supper alone. Karen used half a stick of butter on her baked potato, but Julie didn't have the energy to argue with her.

Squirting more catsup on her meat loaf, Julie only half-listened to Karen as she tattled on various day care kids. Her mind kept racing from one worry to another—her dad's brooding state of mind, her mom's total exhaustion, her own indecision about the cafeteria job, Monica's constant teasing about Julie's used jeans and sack lunches. . . .

Half an hour later, Julie and Karen were in the upstairs bathroom when their mom came home. "I'm back," she called up the stairs.

"Be down soon!" Julie shouted over Karen's splashing. "Hurry up," she urged, taking the wind-up shark away from Karen and handing her a blue washcloth instead.

"Give that back!" Karen screamed, splashing soapy water on the wallpaper. "I'm going to tell! I'm going to tell!"

"Oh, hush." Julie threw back the gray plastic shark.

Fuming, she studied her scowling little sister. In just two weeks, she'd noticed a change in Karen. She'd always been sweet and cooperative, but after bossing around half a dozen small kids, she'd turned into a miniature tyrant. Julie didn't much like the change.

Another fifteen minutes passed before Julie persuaded Karen to scrub and get out of the tub. Then, in a flurry, Julie squeezed out Karen's dripping ponytail, hung up her towel, rinsed the grimy tub, and hurried downstairs. After waiting all evening, she was ready to burst with her good news.

Coming around the corner into the living room, Julie slid to a stop. Her mom was home, all right—at least technically. She lay in the flowered recliner, her feet up and her eyes closed. Holding her breath, Julie tiptoed closer to make sure. Yup, those soft, fluttery sounds were snores.

Swallowing her disappointment, Julie backed away. Her mom had been working nonstop since five a.m. She couldn't wake her up just to tell her about the tryouts. The news would wait another day, Julie supposed. She might as well go read another chapter of *Charlotte's Web* to Karen, then tuck her in.

Turning to leave, Julie paused and studied her dozing

mother. The fine lines in her face were deep furrows now, and she frowned even in her sleep. Julie twisted her damp shirt tail. If *only* there was something more she could do.

Even though Julie sympathized with her mom's exhaustion, the situation at home was getting to her. More and more, Julie felt invisible.

If she disappeared in a puff of smoke someday, would anybody even notice?

*Chapter 5*

# Bad News

Julie waited for the right moment all week to make her announcement. However, the only time the day care kids were gone, her mom was either asleep, doing bookkeeping, or talking urgently with her dad in whispered conferences.

Besides, being chosen for the cheerleading squad had presented another big problem—money. Or the lack of it.

Julie mulled over the situation on Friday morning as she waited for the bus. She glanced heavenward, as if expecting an answer, but the morning sky showed only unbroken grey clouds.

To her dismay, she'd discovered the day before that being a cheerleader cost money—money she didn't have and couldn't ask her parents for. The rental and cleaning fee for her uniform was twenty dollars, and the red and white matching saddle shoes were forty dollars. She was expected to produce the money within a week.

Shivering in the chill, Julie climbed aboard the bus and plopped down on a ripped, vinyl seat. Monica leaned over the seat behind her.

Julie gritted her teeth and freed her hair from under Monica's elbow. "What's up?" she asked.

"This." With a flourish, Monica presented her with a hand-addressed, pink envelope covered with heart stickers. "Ta-da! It's time for my annual birthday sleep-over."

"I'd almost forgotten," Julie said, brightening.

Monica could be a real pain sometimes, but she threw terrific parties. There was always enough pizza to feed an army, half a dozen movies for the VCR, and ping-pong and games in the rec room if they got bored. Best of all, her mom never made them go to bed until they were ready.

Flipping through her pile of invitations, Monica read the names aloud. Julie whipped around in surprise when she heard Heather Sherman's name. "You're inviting Heather?" she asked. Monica and Heather had been mortal enemies during the first month of the school year.

Monica shrugged. "I know you like her, so I guess she's not *that* bad." Pursing her glossy pink lips, she frowned. "Now that you mention it, I doubt if she could afford much of a birthday present."

Julie's smile froze. A *present.* She'd forgotten.

Turning to look out the window, Julie scraped at the

thick frost on the bottom of the glass. She stuck the envelope in her math book, knowing she'd have to turn down the invitation. She'd never before missed one of Monica's slumber parties, but this year's was out of the question.

No way could she afford a present. With Christmas coming soon, she'd be lucky to afford gifts for her own small family. Biting her lip, Julie opened her social studies book and pretended to study.

At noon, Julie rushed to her locker. Her stomach had been growling since ten o'clock, so her peanut butter and raisin sandwich even sounded mouth-watering. Whipping open her rusty army locker, she peered inside, then kicked it shut.

"Not again!" Turning, she slumped against her locker.

This was the third time that week that her lunch had been stolen. She couldn't believe it. Who would want her stupid sandwich? Probably nobody, she answered herself. There had been a rash of thefts from lockers all fall. Someone's idea of a joke, Julie figured.

"Some locker," she muttered, reaching inside to grab her denim jacket. "Why can't we have *locks* on our lockers?" Zipping up her jacket, she headed outside.

Underneath the maple trees by the parking lot, Julie leaned against the rough bark and pulled her knees up under her chin. The branches above were filled with silver-white glints of sun.

Her growling stomach churned noisily, reminding her that it had been six hours since her oatmeal that morning. Julie knew she couldn't go without lunch forever, but she refused to report the thefts to the principal.

Carrying her lunch was bad enough. She wouldn't open herself up to more ridicule by having the principal check into the thefts. However, at this rate, she could starve to death if she didn't do anything.

Enough was enough.

If she didn't want to starve, she'd better check into that cafeteria job. If she could *earn* free lunches, it wouldn't be charity, so her dad shouldn't mind. Even so, Julie didn't plan to tell him about the cafeteria job for a while. He was upset enough right now by her mom's new job.

By the time she got home after school, Julie was weak with hunger. She swiped the last three broken sugar cookies from the jar on the counter, stuffing them into her mouth before any ravenous kids spotted her.

Sighing, she stacked her schoolbooks on top of the refrigerator where no one could reach them, then forced herself to go help with the afternoon snack. Julie rubbed her throbbing forehead. Sometimes it took every ounce of strength she had to face the hordes of screeching kids after school.

How did her mom stand it, day after day?

That night at supper, Julie wolfed down whole wheat pancakes as fast as her mom refilled the platter. Meatless meals had become common lately, but Julie liked the french toast, grilled cheese sandwiches, and casseroles. As long as the food was hot and there was plenty of it, that's all that mattered to her. Especially on the days her lunch sack disappeared.

Supper was eaten in silence, as so many of their meals were these days. It wasn't until Julie had polished off her seventh pancake and leaned back, groaning, that she realized how thick the tension was. Her dad's plate was still full; he'd eaten only half a pancake.

"You feeling all right, Dad?" Julie tried not to sound anxious.

Her dad dropped his fork and smiled wryly. "Your mother is certainly a whiz at making a meal out of nothing," he said. "Not many women can stretch a dollar like that. It's ironic, though, that the farmers who grow the food don't have enough money to buy it." He scraped his chair back from the table, then got a couple of antacids out of the cupboard.

Julie's heart ached for her dad. If only she could say something to make it easier. She knew her mom was afraid that her dad had an ulcer, but he had point-blank refused to see a doctor.

Julie's dad hugged her mom where she stood at the old gas stove, flipping pancakes, then pulled his seed corn cap low on his forehead. "I need to get back out to the field—at least while it's still mine."

He trudged out the back way, letting the screen door slam behind him. He passed by the window, shoulders slumped under his coveralls, on his way to the pickup. Outside, the shadows yawned and stretched, as the last faint color of the day faded.

At least the weather was decent, Julie thought. Lots of times they'd had snow by Halloween, but it had been in the fifties all week. With any luck, he'd be able to get the whole crop out.

After turning off the stove, Julie's mom collapsed in her chair at the table. At that moment, Karen jumped up to go watch TV, twirling her baton behind her. Linda McGregor watched her younger daughter disappear into the living room, then shook her head sadly.

"You know, I hardly ever have time alone with Karen anymore. I *miss* it. Working at home seemed like such a good idea at first."

"It *is* hard to find a quiet minute alone these days."

Her mom laid her head on her folded arms. "I was starving a minute ago, but now I'm too tired to eat."

"Here, let me. I should have cooked the last round so you could eat sooner. I'm sorry." Julie buttered three pancakes for her mom, then covered them with maple syrup. "Try these. You'll feel better if you eat."

"Thanks, Honey." She chewed the first bite slowly, then smiled and ate faster. "This *does* taste good, meat or no meat."

"I think so too. Dad probably doesn't mind that much either."

"He's not upset about the food." Her mom paused, then plunged ahead. "He heard from the banker this week. Mr. Curtis thinks he may have found a buyer for our eighty acres."

"Already? Isn't that kind of sudden?"

"That's what I said. Evidently the banker had someone in mind all along." This time her mother hesitated longer, then laid down her fork and folded her hands in her lap. "However, there's one big problem with the sale, and there's no reason to put off telling you."

Julie held her breath. The only sound in the dining room was the ticking of the wall clock. "What's the problem?"

"This buyer's offer isn't enough to pay off our bank loan. It will still leave us quite a bit short."

"What does that mean exactly?"

Her mom gripped Julie's hands in her own. "It means we have to sell our house and the acre it sits on."

"Our house?" Julie jerked back. "Sell our *house?"* she repeated. There had to be some mistake! The house had been in her dad's family for three generations. They couldn't sell it!

Methodically, Julie shredded her paper napkin. The pieces fluttered unnoticed to the floor. "Mom, what are we going to do?"

Julie's mom looked Julie square in the eye. "Frankly,

Honey, I don't know. Maybe another offer—a better one—will be made. But whatever happens, I *do* know one thing, and I don't want you to ever forget it." She put a hand under Julie's chin. "God hasn't forgotten us. He will meet our needs if we continue to trust Him."

Julie nodded, but she wondered how in the world her mom could still believe that. Especially now, since it appeared they'd soon lose the roof over their heads.

That night, Julie tossed and turned in bed as she listened to the corn picker in the field across the road. Her dad had worked till ten or eleven o'clock the past few nights, since rain was predicted for the weekend. Julie hated to admit it, but it was easier having him work late these days than hanging around the house, depressed and angry.

It was getting hard enough, Julie admitted, to fight her *own* depression.

It was tough being teased about her sack lunches, wearing secondhand clothes, and then turning down Monica's invitation because she couldn't afford a present. And what about the money she owed for her cheerleading shoes and uniform? She'd already received two reminders about that.

The holidays didn't look any brighter, Julie thought glumly, curling into a ball. There would be little money for gifts, she was sure of that. And with the way her dad's stomach hurt, he was in no mood to be jolly.

Her mom was so frazzled these days that she hardly

talked to Julie anymore. They did very little together except work. Julie hadn't even told her mom about winning a place on the cheerleading squad! Instead of being happy news, it just presented another problem.

Of course, the worst thing was the thought of selling their house. Julie sat up and crawled to the end of her bed near the window. Leaning on the window ledge, she watched the picker across the road. The headlights swept across the field as the churning dust boiled in huge clouds around the giant machine.

Overhead, a frosty moon peeked out from behind a thin cloud. The moonlight bleached the outbuildings below a dead white.

The headlights swept a wide arc as the picker turned at the end of the row. Julie couldn't imagine her dad doing anything except what he was doing right at the minute. She couldn't imagine living anywhere else except in their farmhouse. Still, her mom said they'd probably have to sell out.

Julie wrapped her shivering arms around herself. Regardless of what her mom believed, it looked like God was going to let them down.

Leaning her forehead against the cool glass, Julie wrestled with her doubts. She'd been brought up to believe that the Bible was God's Word and could be trusted. And it claimed that God would supply their needs—no ifs, ands, or buts.

So it really came down to one question: would she trust God or not?

Julie gazed over the trees, silver in their dried leaves, into the clear night sky above. The shining rhinestone stars glittered ice cold, and the moon sparkled like a shimmering silver dollar.

A quiet peace settled over her heart. *Surely* if God could set the stars and moon in the sky, and keep the planets revolving around the sun, He could handle whatever problem the McGregor family had.

It was a question of believing, Julie realized, believing and trusting God, no matter how bad things looked at the time. It was something her mom had known for ages. Julie decided it was time to learn that for herself.

Shivering, she crawled back under her blanket.

*Chapter 6*

# *Tough Decisions*

Shivering, Julie crawled further under her electric blanket, grateful for a warm, quiet place to study for her test. Since their furnace oil was so expensive, they weren't heating the upstairs bedrooms this winter.

Her blanket pulled up to her chin, Julie closed her eyes and tried to list all the early American Indian tribes. Halfway through her list, she dozed off to sleep.

Shaking herself awake, Julie stared out the frosty window at the cold November night. Soft, far-flung stars appeared just out of reach. For the past two weeks, her family had lived in limbo, waiting for the ax to fall. Then their eighty acres had been sold to someone from a neighboring state. The offer had been disappointing, not nearly enough to pay off the bank loan.

Julie still hadn't told anyone about the cheerleading tryouts. If only she could come up with the money for her uniform and shoes! Then she could make her big announcement. Without the money, though, Julie knew she was left with little choice.

Her mom was still exhausted from running her Country Care Center, but she didn't complain or waver in her faith that God would provide for them. Julie continued to carry her lunch, but she no longer left it in her locker. Instead, she stuffed a sandwich in her purse and kept it with her.

One thing *had* changed during the past two weeks, though. Her dad had grown worse.

Julie turned the blanket control up to "HI," then scrunched the blanket up closer around her shoulders. Her dad tried not to show it, but she knew he was sicker. He ate antacids like candy, drank milk by the gallon, and ate small meals throughout the day, instead of his usual three squares. But it wasn't helping.

Often Julie had come down in the early morning to find him huddled on the couch, the heating pad pressed tightly to his stomach. Just the morning before, Julie had mustered the courage to ask if he shouldn't go see Dr. Sanders.

He'd patted her hand, then said, "It's just indigestion. Anyway, doctors and medicine cost money."

Julie hadn't believed the "indigestion" story, but she hadn't argued with him, either. Anything costing extra money was "out," as she well knew.

Chilled in spite of her blanket, Julie decided to make some hot chocolate. Down in the kitchen, she reached into the cupboard for the cocoa, but halted at the agitated voices coming from the dining room.

"Roy, you've got to stop ignoring this problem." Her mom's voice was gentle, but firm. "I haven't nagged you about it, but I just can't keep quiet anymore."

"Honey, you worry too much."

"No, I don't. In fact, I try very hard *not* to worry, but this is too serious to let go."

"Honest, I'm OK. Just a little upset stomach. The flu's going around, you know."

Julie held her breath, her fingers gripping the Hershey's cocoa can. She felt guilty for eavesdropping, but *knowing* bad news was easier to handle than all the secrecy.

"This is no flu." Her mom's voice was persistent. "I came in while you were sick in the bathroom. Don't pretend you don't know what I'm talking about." Her voice dropped, and Julie could barely make out her words over the steady hum of the refrigerator. "You were throwing up blood just now."

Julie clapped a hand over her mouth to stifle a gasp. There was total silence as the kitchen clock ticked off ten seconds.

"I'll call the doctor tomorrow," her dad agreed, "but it's probably nothing."

"It's probably a bleeding ulcer. Ignoring it will only

make it worse." Julie's mom hesitated, then added, "When you're in town tomorrow, there's someone else I'd like you to see."

"Who's that?"

"I've talked to some of the mothers who bring their kids here. They said there's an agency now in New Hampton where farmers in trouble can get some help."

"What kind of help?" Julie's dad asked suspiciously.

"Well, financial advice, for one thing, and career counseling," her mom said brightly. "Also some emotional support. You could talk to someone about your problems, instead of keeping them inside and making ulcers. I believe the counseling's free."

"I don't care if it's free!" Julie's dad exploded. "I have no intention of talking to a shrink! I won't be seen coming out of some counseling office!" He pounded his fist on the table. "And career advice would be worthless. I'm just a farmer—that's all I know how to do."

Blood pounded in Julie's ears until she feared her head would burst. Karen's giggles over a TV comedy show in the living room seemed grotesquely out of place.

Finally Julie's mom spoke, and Julie could hear the tears in her voice. "Roy, you've *got* to talk to somebody. You won't even talk to me anymore! No matter how much we want to, we can't live in the past. We have to look to the future."

"What future?"

Julie's mom let out a long, shaky breath. "I don't know what the future holds any more than you do. But God knows, and we can trust Him."

Her dad sighed. "I know that, even if it doesn't seem that way." Julie ached at the defeat in her dad's voice. "I'm used to being on my own," he continued, "answering to no one but myself. I can't stand the idea of finding a different line of work, with some boss always looking over my shoulder."

"I understand. Let's take one thing at a time, and see the doctor first. We need to get this ulcer—or whatever it is—under control. And then . . ."

Turning, Julie tiptoed in stocking feet from the kitchen, without making her hot chocolate. She'd lost her appetite, as well as her incentive to study.

It wasn't the first time. She couldn't concentrate on her school work. Quarterly grades would be released soon. For the first time in her life, Julie was afraid to see her report card.

Upstairs in her room, Julie paused at the card table in the corner, where her fishing village puzzle was taking shape. She needed a break from her worries, if only for a minute.

She arranged and rearranged a handful of speckled gray puzzle pieces, trying to make the sign that hung over the cottage door. Blocking out the memory of her parents' conversation, she studied the box lid, then concentrated on fitting the pieces together, turning them this way and that. Five minutes later, when the completed sign section read "Ravenswhip Cove," Julie went downstairs to take her shower.

Hopping on the ancient bathroom scales, Julie blinked in surprise. She'd lost seven pounds since school started. No wonder her jeans were hanging so baggy lately.

I ought to write a best-selling weight-loss book, Julie thought wryly. *How to Worry Your Weight Away.* The combination of stolen lunches, baby-sitting after school, less meat, and more worry was an effective diet.

Julie stood under the steamy shower and closed her eyes, trying to relax. But the memory of her dad's defeated voice crowded out all her other thoughts. With the loan due in a few weeks, and no work lined up for the winter, he'd have to do something.

And soon.

Toweling her hair dry a few minutes later, Julie admitted that she herself had some decisions to make. She'd put them off, hoping the problems would go away. But they hadn't.

For one thing, she didn't get enough to eat for lunch, although she had assured her parents otherwise. And she was sick to death of those squished peanut butter sandwiches every day. Most times it was barely an hour before she was starving again.

Julie ran a wide-toothed plastic comb through her wet

hair and wiped the steam from the bathroom mirror. Sighing, she decided she'd better swallow her pride and ask Mrs. Oswald about the cafeteria job. It would be honest work—not charity—plus she'd be able to eat hot lunch again with her friends. Cooking in the cafeteria might be embarrassing, but the Lord was providing her with free hot lunches, and she knew she should be grateful. Maybe if she'd told someone about her problems before this, an answer would have come sooner.

She'd talk to the principal the very next day, Julie decided. If only her other decisions were as easy to make.

After hanging up her wet towels, she perched on the edge of the tub. The basketball games started in three weeks, on the first of December. Cheerleading practices were scheduled after school the following week. She'd hoped and prayed that the uniform and shoe money would magically appear, but it hadn't happened.

Tears welled up and spilled over, making dark pink blotches on her light pink pajamas. Julie had worked so hard to earn her place on the cheerleading squad. But her help was needed at home after school, there wasn't any extra money, and that was that.

Julie wiped her reddened eyes, then splashed her face with ice-cold water. Her parents mustn't suspect she'd been crying. They had enough to worry about. She'd have to handle these problems herself.

Julie stared into the mirror, then nodded with determination. She'd march into the principal's office first thing the next morning and do two things.

First, she'd apply for the cafeteria job. Second, she'd resign from the cheerleading squad.

*Chapter 7*

# *Trusting in the Dark*

Before she could lose her resolve the next morning, Julie squared her shoulders and marched into the office. "Could I see Mrs. Oswald, please?" she asked the school secretary. "I'm Julie McGregor."

"Just a moment." The secretary disappeared into the principal's private office, then reappeared. "You can go in."

Julie stared at the ornate brass name plate, counted to ten, then pushed open the heavy door. Mrs. Oswald sat at her desk, hunched over a thick report. Her beehive hairdo leaned at an odd angle. Standing, she pulled a folding chair near her desk.

"Come in and sit down, Julie. What can I do for you?"

"Two things, actually." Perched on the edge of her chair,

Julie stared at the checked carpet. *Oh, Lord, help me get the words out,* she prayed silently. Taking a deep breath, she looked Mrs. Oswald in the eye. "I'm here to resign from the basketball cheerleading squad. I won't be able to participate." She chewed her bottom lip, hoping Mrs. Oswald wouldn't press for details.

The older woman stuck her pencil into her beehive, then nodded. "I'm sorry to hear that. Are you absolutely sure?"

"I'm sure." Julie gripped the edge of her metal chair. "My second reason for coming here is this: Can I still work in the cafeteria in exchange for free lunches?"

"I think that can be arranged. Let me talk to the cooks and see. I'll get back to you as soon as possible."

"Thank you." Julie stood, stiffening her wobbly knees, then held out her hand to Mrs. Oswald. "Thank you for seeing me."

"You're welcome. That's why I'm here." Mrs. Oswald's long fingers held Julie's hand in an iron grip. "Is there anything else I can do for you? I have time if you want to talk."

"I appreciate that," Julie said, extracting her hand, "but I have to get to class."

"I understand." Mrs. Oswald held open the door for her.

Outside the office, Julie hurried around the corner and leaned weakly against the green cement wall. She realized what she'd just given up, and her knees threatened to buckle. Waves of disappointment washed over Julie as if to drown her. Winning a place on the cheerleading squad had been a dream come true for her. Giving that up had been one of the hardest things she'd ever done.

Still, she reminded herself, it was nothing compared to the sacrifices her parents had to make. Her heart heavy, Julie headed to her first class.

It wasn't until third period English that an office aide delivered Mrs. Oswald's note. Blushing at the curious stares of the students, Julie opened the folded paper and read: "It's all arranged. Remain in the cafeteria after your lunch period instead of going to study hall. Mrs. Johansen will train you today. Good luck!" Mrs. Oswald's signature was scrawled in bold letters across the bottom.

In the lunch line at noon, Julie's mouth watered at the smell of the sloppy joes. Actually, Julie didn't care *what* was for lunch, as long as it wasn't a peanut butter sandwich.

In a whisper, she explained to Heather about the cafeteria job she was starting that day. "I'll join you in study hall later if I have time," she added.

Although she tried to sound casual, Julie was nervous. She didn't even know Mrs. Johansen, the head cook. What would be expected of her? Julie imagined they'd work ahead on the next day's lunch. Although she helped out at home, Julie didn't have a lot of cooking experience. She hoped that wouldn't be crucial to her job.

She needn't have worried, Julie thought, half an hour later.

Mrs. Johansen's "training" consisted of showing her where the stained dish rags, broom, and dustpan were stored. Julie's new job wasn't even in the kitchen—it was in the lunch room. She had to wipe off the tables and chairs after lunch, then sweep the cafeteria.

*I'm grateful for the job. I really am,* Julie tried to convince herself.

But, to be honest, she hoped none of her classmates walked by and saw her. She'd get more ridicule for her clean-up job than she had for carrying a sack lunch.

In science class that afternoon, however, all worry about her new job vanished when the latest tests were handed back. Julie took one look at the D on her paper and nearly fainted.

She checked the name at the top of the page, sure that the test belonged to someone else. She'd never received anything lower than a B in this class.

But there was no mistake—it was her exam.

Ashamed, Julie slid the test into her purple pocket folder. She'd have to buckle down and bring her grade back up. No matter what was happening at home, she'd have to concentrate better.

A threatening black cloud hung over Julie all afternoon. The last thing she wanted to do when she dragged off the school bus was to entertain a bunch of unruly kids. On days like this, when school left her in a turmoil, she missed the old peace and quiet the most.

The bus roared away down the winding ribbon of a dusty road. Aware of faint honking, Julie studied the sky until she spotted the V-formation of geese in the distance. She shivered, although the sun peered through a break in the clouds, and hunched her coat collar higher against the blustery wind.

Near the back door, Julie peered under the lilac bush. The milk bowl was there, nearly empty, a curled leaf floating on the surface. The gray kitten, its stomach distended to the breaking point, stretched, yawned, rolled over, and went back to sleep. Julie grinned. It didn't take her mom long to tame a wild kitten.

Julie glanced around the farm yard, trying to take mental Polaroid pictures of her home for the future. Just then a slight movement in the machine shed caught Julie's eye. She frowned and squinted. Some day care kid was out there playing in the cab of the blue pickup.

She dropped her denim bag and headed for the shed. Those kids! If her mom had told them once, she'd told them a million times: Stay away from the outbuildings. There were too many things they could break, and too many ways to get hurt.

Entering the spacious shed, Julie waited for her eyes to adjust to the dimness. Then she realized she'd made a mistake. That was no child in the truck—it was her dad. Motionless, he rested his arms on the steering wheel and stared straight ahead at the shed's unpainted wall.

It scared her, seeing him out there alone, just sitting. Julie hesitated, then backed up slowly. Abruptly, he turned and spotted her.

Her dad opened the squeaky door, then climbed stiffly down from the cab. “Hi, Honey. I didn’t hear the school bus.”

“Where have you been?” Julie asked, surprised to see him in a dress shirt and tie.

He shuffled across the dirt floor to where she stood in the doorway. “Oh, I paid a visit to Dr. Sanders this afternoon,” he said casually.

“What did he say?”

“Just that I work too hard.” Her dad’s laugh sounded forced.

“That’s all?” Julie was skeptical, recalling the conversation she’d overheard the night before. “Well, I have a small ulcer too.” Her dad dug in his coat pocket for a small white pharmacy sack. “The doctor prescribed some medicine and gave me a bland diet to follow.”

“Is that enough? Didn’t he want you in the hospital?”

“Actually, I’ve been there already. This afternoon I had an ‘upper GI series’ done at the hospital.”

“What’s that?” Julie tried to sound calm and matter-of-fact, like her mom.

“Oh, you swallow this stuff called barium—it’s a pink chalky liquid—and they X-ray your stomach afterwards. That’s how the doctor knew I had an ulcer.”

Julie swallowed hard and wrapped her arms around his waist. "Does it hurt?"

"Some, but with the diet and medicine, it should be better soon." He squeezed her hard. "Don't worry."

Just then a long, shiny maroon car coasted smoothly up the driveway. The tinted windows kept the driver's face in deep shadow. After parking, a plump woman emerged, leather briefcase in hand.

"Just what I need." Julie's dad wiped a roughened hand over his weary face. "It's Mrs. Dann, the realtor. She's listing the house today."

Arm in arm, Julie and her dad crossed the windy yard, while a couple of crows watched from the plowed garden. Arriving at the back door as Mrs. Dann pressed the bell, Julie picked up her book bag before the realtor could trip over it.

"Hello, Mr. McGregor. Quite a stiff wind today," she chirped. Her smile pushed her chubby pink cheeks even higher on her face.

Julie studied the realtor's round face and artfully arranged hairdo. It might be a breezy day, but Mrs. Dann's heavily sprayed hair hadn't even fluttered. It squatted on her head like a gray helmet. It would take a tornado to budge it.

Following her dad and Mrs. Dann inside, Julie quickly corralled the day care kids. With Karen's help, she organized them into circles of "Drop the Handkerchief" and

"Duck, Duck, Goose." Although there was a lot of running and squealing, they stayed put in the living room so her parents could talk in the dining room.

As she held a teething toddler on her lap, Julie was glad the baby's wailing had drowned out the conversation. She couldn't bear to hear them discuss what price to ask for the house, or how to dispose of the farm machinery in the sheds.

If she didn't actually hear it, Julie could still pretend it wasn't happening.

But it was real, she thought an hour later as she watched Mrs. Dann from the living room window. Camera slung around her neck, the chunky woman snapped several shots of their house, then planted an orange "For Sale" sign by the road. It read: "If *you're* looking for it, *we've* got it—at DANN REALTY."

Supper that night was somber. With the "For Sale" sign in the front yard, Julie could no longer deny that they were about to lose everything.

From the corner of her eye, Julie studied her parents, who stared into their plates. The lines in her dad's face had deepened into creases, and her mom had permanent black circles under her eyes.

Her dad pushed away his nearly full plate. "I've never been so exhausted in my life. I think I'd be too tired to eat tonight, even if we had T-bones." Massaging the back of his neck, he shuffled into the living room.

After supper, Julie's mom set another bowl of warmed milk by the back step, then began carrying dirty dishes to the kitchen. "I know it looks bleak, Julie, but we've got to keep trusting God to provide." She squirted dish soap in the sink, then turned and wrapped her arms around Julie. "Sometimes it gets pretty dark before the answer comes. Trusting is hardest then."

Julie nodded. It seemed unreal that, once the house sold, they'd move to town. She couldn't imagine having no barn full of cats, no grove of trees, no privacy, and no space.

"What are we going to do?" Julie asked.

Her mom gazed back steadily. "The only thing we *can* do—wait. It's in God's hands now. He'll do what's best."

She walked over to the refrigerator, covered with Karen's art work, day care menus, and family snapshots, all held in place with various magnets. She pointed to the words on one magnet: "'God gives the best to those who leave the choice to Him.'"

"Do you believe that?" Julie asked.

"Oh, yes," her mom said. "Over the years, I've seen it happen time and time again."

Julie nodded, envying her mom's strong, unwavering faith. If only she could be that sure herself! Perhaps in time, Julie hoped. Until then, she'd just have to keep trusting in the dark.

*Chapter 8*

# *'Tis the Season*

The next two weeks flew by, and Julie barely had time to sleep, let alone worry. Her rock collection for science was due, complete with a twenty-page report. Her daily cafeteria job used up the one study hall she'd had. After school she helped baby-sit, then practiced piano music in the evening for the church's Christmas program.

So far their house hadn't sold, although Mrs. Dann had shown their home to several families. Those had been rough times, as critical strangers checked out the rooms and snooped in the closets. Some discussed repapering the faded dining room walls, while others wanted to rip out the worn shag carpet.

It made Julie want to scream, "You have no *right* to talk about our house this way!" But she didn't. She was polite and helpful on the outside, while it tore her apart inside to imagine another family living in their house.

The weekend before Thanksgiving, Julie's mom bought a chicken to roast for the holiday, rather than a turkey or ham, but no one seemed to mind. Not being able to afford a turkey was the least of their problems, Julie thought.

Having no money for a birthday present bothered her a lot more. Monica's slumber party was just a week away, but Julie had already turned down the invitation. She hated being left out, but she didn't see how she could go and not take a present. As it was, she'd be lucky if her meager savings covered the cost of her Christmas shopping.

On Friday she withdrew the last twenty-five dollars from her savings account. On Saturday morning, with it tucked in her purse, Julie caught a ride to New Hampton with her dad. She always did her Christmas shopping before Thanksgiving, when merchandise wasn't so picked over.

"Thanks for bringing me," Julie said as they pulled up to the mall entrance. Giving her dad a quick kiss, she climbed down from the truck.

"I'll meet you back here in two hours," he reminded her. Waving, he drove away to run errands of his own.

Inside the mall, Julie's sagging spirits rose in spite of herself. Christmas carols blared over the P.A. system, and the decorations were better than ever this year. A towering white castle was surrounded by three displays of animated penguins, ice fishing. Julie never told her friends, but she secretly loved the gaudy decorations. For a brief time each year, it turned the mall into a place of magic.

Smiling, Julie marched down the mall, humming along with the music: "Let it snow, let it snow, let it snow." She decided, for the moment, to put out of her mind the sale of their home and her dad's ulcer, and to let the holiday spirit fill her.

But by the time she'd trudged through Wal-Mart, Smith's Music, Toys for Kids, and the Country Craft store an hour later, Julie's spirits had drooped. She hadn't bought a single gift yet, although she'd found dozens of gifts her family would love. If only she could afford them! Just one sweater for her mother or a big stuffed animal for Karen would have taken her entire twenty-five dollars.

Discouraged, Julie slumped down on a bench near one of the penguin displays.

In addition to presents for her family, there would be a gift exchange with her Sunday-school class, a small donation for both bus drivers' gifts, plus Julie wanted to buy something for Heather. It would stretch her twenty-five dollars mighty thin.

Julie glanced at her watch and gasped. In just forty-five minutes, her dad would be waiting at the entrance. There was no use sitting and crying over what she couldn't afford—she'd just have to be more creative.

Straightening her shoulders, she marched back to the toy

store where she'd seen some horse models on sale. Karen would love two of them. Julie could make two little horse blankets to go with them.

Trying to view it as a challenge, Julie rushed from store to store, hunting for bargains. She purchased a glass jar with a wooden lid for her mother, to be filled with chocolate-covered mints. For her dad, she found a small screwdriver/wrench set on sale in the hardware store. It would be handy to keep in the glove compartment of the car.

Julie wanted something special for Heather, but nothing she saw struck her as "just right." Then, when browsing through the Keepsake Quilting shop, she found the perfect gift. There among the rag dolls, quilted bunnies, and stuffed chenille bears, was a kitten curled up in a quilted basket. Like Julie, Heather loved cats, so it would be the perfect present.

Julie glanced at the price tag and frowned. It cost four dollars more than she had.

Sighing, she set it back down and was nearly out of the store when she snapped her fingers. There was a small wicker basket under her bed at home that she could use. Retracing her steps, she approached the lady at the cash register.

"Um, excuse me," Julie said, "could I buy that quilted kitten, but without the basket?"

"Which kitten?" the lady asked. She followed Julie to

the back of the store, where she examined the calico kitten. "I guess that would be fine. Without the basket, I'll cut the price of the kitten to $4.50."

"I'll take it," Julie said. She pulled out her last crumpled dollar bills while the woman wrapped the kitten in tissue paper.

Then, humming "It Came Upon a Midnight Clear," Julie raced to the mall entrance. Her dad hadn't arrived yet, so Julie sat down to catch her breath. She thought about each of her purchases with real satisfaction. The gifts might not be expensive, but her family would enjoy them.

Just then Monica's mother pulled up to the curb. Monica and her sister, Terri, climbed out. Waving as the car drove off, Monica and Terri then pushed through the crowd to the mall door and slipped inside.

"Whew! It's freezing out there!" Monica unzipped her leather jacket. "What are you doing here, Julie?"

"Christmas shopping." Julie pointed to her purchases on the bench. "I like to do mine early."

"Me, too." Monica patted her bulging lavender purse. "My list is all made out. I'm buying Mom a mini-blender for the kitchen, and dad needs a new camera. He lost his on vacation last summer." Leaning over, she tried to peer into Julie's sacks. "What did you get your parents?"

"Um, I didn't find them anything yet," Julie lied, holding her sacks close.

Her face grew warm, recalling the inexpensive gifts

SHOP

she'd bought on sale. Julie stared at the wet dirty floor. She felt guilty for lying, yet she just couldn't tell Monica what she'd bought.

Monica shook back her hair, and her silver earrings danced. "I'm buying party decorations too," she added, leaning close to Julie's face. "Are you *sure* you can't come? My birthday party won't be the same without you. I had thought, by inviting everyone so early, there'd be no problem."

"I know, but—well, I wish I could. It just didn't work out this year." Julie stumbled over her words. Looking up, she spotted their blue-and-white pickup. "There's Dad. Gotta go." With relief, she pushed open the glass door and ran to the truck.

"Hi, Dad." Climbing into the cab, Julie piled her packages between them, then stared silently out the window. After hearing what gifts Monica intended to buy, Julie's presents seemed so cheap by comparison.

Slumping down on the cold plastic seat, Julie knew she shouldn't care. Her mom had told them a thousand times over the years that "it's the thought that counts," anyway.

Julie believed that, and yet . . .

At home that afternoon, Julie found the tiny wicker basket beneath her bed when she hid her packages. After lining the basket with a scrap of pink gingham, Julie added the quilted kitten, then grinned. Heather would just *love* it.

However, her joy slowly faded. If only she could have afforded another gift—one for Monica's birthday party. Julie knew that all her friends were going, even Heather. Julie hated feeling left out, but without a gift, she wouldn't go.

Sliding the kitten and basket into a sack, Julie lifted the bedspread and pushed the sack under the bed. Then, pulling the spread back into place, something clicked in Julie's mind. Blinking, she held the edge of the bedspread, trying to capture the thought that flitted around the back of her mind.

Then she remembered.

She'd seen the bears in the craft shop with other handmade animals. The small stuffed bears had been made out of worn chenille, a soft material with little bumps all over it.

"Just like the old pink bedspread in the linen closet!"

Julie's eyes opened wide. Why not make one of those chenille bears for Monica's birthday gift? It couldn't be too hard.

Eyes closed, Julie formed a mental picture of the six-inch bears she'd seen. The eyes and nose were embroidered on the face, she recalled, and a small red heart was sewn on the bear's chest. A red ribbon had been tied at the neck.

Julie raced down the stairs to the basement, where her mom was loading the washing machine with towels.

"Mom, can I have that old pink bedspread in the linen closet?"

"Isn't your electric blanket working?"

"It's not for my bed." Julie cleaned the fuzz from the dryer's lint trap. "In fact, I wondered if I could cut up the bedspread to make something with it."

Her mom poured a lid full of blue detergent in the washer, then nodded. "That old bedspread has been in the closet for years, and no one's wanted it. Sure, go ahead."

"Thanks!"

Julie ran upstairs and pulled down the chenille bedspread from the top shelf of the bathroom closet. Large areas of the spread were worn so thin she could see through it. However, near the bottom, the bumpy material was good as new. Just perfect for her bear.

That night Julie made a bear pattern from a grocery sack, then cut out the material. She hand-sewed the front and back together. Careful to keep her tiny stitches uniform, she worked her way around one arm, up and around the head and ears, then down the other side.

The next afternoon after church, Julie gathered thread, black and red embroidery floss, and stuffing. While her mom read and her dad and Karen napped, Julie sewed. Two hours later, she'd stuffed the bear, embroidered the face and heart, and tied the red ribbon around the neck.

"Not bad," Julie said, "if I do say so myself."

Her mom glanced up from her book. "That's beautiful, Honey. Monica will love it."

"I hope so," Julie said, doubt beginning to creep in.

It wasn't a store-bought gift like Monica was used to, but these stuffed animals *were* popular in the stores this year. Julie studied the bear with a critical eye. Maybe Monica wouldn't even know it was homemade. If she didn't guess, Julie sure wasn't going to tell her.

Julie lined a small box with white tissue paper, then laid the bear inside. "Can I call Monica?" she asked.

Her mom nodded without looking up. Julie went to make the call, rehearsing her lines on the way to the phone.

It rang four times before Monica picked up the phone. Julie reeled off her planned speech all in one breath. "I had to rearrange my plans for next weekend and I wondered if I could change my mind and still come to your party, if it's all right with you, that is, if it isn't too late," she finished, her throat tight.

"You can come? Really? That's great!"

Julie leaned against the table in relief. "OK. See you tomorrow." Hanging up, Julie cartwheeled through the kitchen, kicking the refrigerator, then went to clean up her sewing scraps.

Her mom leaned back in the recliner, an afghan over her legs. "All set for Monica's party?"

"Yup. I'm so glad I just happened to see those bears in the craft shop, and then I thought of this old bedspread."

"I'm glad it worked out too. However, I doubt that you 'just happened' to think of the old bedspread. It wasn't just a coincidence."

"What do you mean?"

"God knew you needed a gift for Monica's party. He provided for your need in an unexpected way." She smiled and tucked the afghan around her stockinged feet.

Julie stroked the pink chenille bear, wondering if her mom could be right. She had to admit she would never have thought of making a gift herself. Then, praying a silent "Thank You, Lord," Julie began wrapping the birthday present.

*Chapter 9*

# *Keeping Secrets*

That evening, Julie headed to the barn with a light step, carrying food and water for the cats. Although nothing had really changed, at least she could go to Monica's party. She was grateful for that.

In the dark barn, Julie ignored the eerie murmur of pigeons roosting above in the rafters as she maneuvered along the rough, splintery wall. When she found the light switch, she flipped it up. A faint yellow light illuminated the center of the barn, but left the corners in deep shadow.

Julie spotted the new stray, crouched under the hay rack. "Here, kitty, kitty." She held out some food in her hand, but the gray kitten eyed her suspiciously. It remained crouched, ears down, tail flat.

Shrugging, Julie dumped the ice from the water dishes and refilled them. Then she spread the dry cat food in the feeding trough her dad had built. Fifteen cats shot out from the nooks and crannies of the barn and hayloft and lined up, head to head, at the trough.

Squatting down, Julie sadly stroked each head in turn.

She'd avoided thinking much about it until now, but if they moved to town, they couldn't take along fifteen cats. What would become of them? Julie doubted that the new owners would want all the strays that had been dumped by the side of the road.

Her reddened fingers were growing numb in the cold, so Julie rose and turned off the barn light. She trudged across the frozen yard, illuminated by the moon in the harsh, night sky. There'd be time enough to worry about the cats when the house sold.

*If* it sold, Julie reminded herself.

Back in the garage, Julie slipped out of her old coat, hung it on a metal hook, then hurried inside to the warm kitchen. Her mom was on the phone, and Julie caught the tail end of her sentence.

" . . . had no idea she'd done that. I wish she hadn't." A moment later her mom added, "She just walked in, Monica. Here she is." Covering the mouthpiece, her mom frowned. "Why didn't you tell us that you made the cheerleading squad and then resigned?"

Julie opened and closed her mouth several times, but no

words came out. That Monica! She had a lot of nerve telling her mom about that. Her parents had enough to worry about. Shrugging, Julie took the phone.

Julie barely heard a word Monica said as she babbled on about her party plans. She was aware that her mom stood nearby, waiting for an answer.

"I'll talk to you tomorrow," Julie finally said, after promising to bring her Trivial Pursuit game to the party. Hanging up, Julie turned slowly.

Her mom leaned against the kitchen counter. "Why, Julie?"

Julie tried to think of a reason that wouldn't upset her mom, but without success. "I made cheerleader a few weeks ago, but I didn't have the money for the uniform rental or the shoes. I needed over sixty dollars, and I couldn't ask you for it."

"Oh, Honey, I'm sorry. If only you'd told me! I'd have found a way to get the money."

"Please don't feel bad." Julie forced a smile. "I don't mind so much anymore. You've got more important things to think about than this."

Julie's mom hugged her close, smoothing her daughter's long hair down the middle of her back. "I just wish . . ." Her voice trailed off sadly.

Julie sighed in agreement. She knew what her mom had almost said, because she wished the very same thing herself.

When the phone rang again, Julie reached for it. "Monica probably forgot something," she said.

However, it wasn't Monica on the line. It was Mrs. Dann. Her hand shaking, Julie gave the phone to her mom. "It's the realtor. She says she has good news for us."

Julie couldn't hear Mrs. Dann's words, but she didn't need to. Watching the color drain from her mom's face, she could guess what the "good news" was.

"Yes, of course, Mrs. Dann. It certainly happened quickly," her mom said. A moment later, she hung up.

Julie felt old, and exhausted, and defeated, and numb. "The house has been sold, hasn't it?" she asked.

Her mom nodded, then collapsed at the table. Staring off into space, she resembled a white marble statue. Her lips barely moved when she said, "Mrs. Dann will be out tomorrow to have us sign some papers."

"Who wants to buy the house?"

"She didn't say."

Julie glanced out the window. "Dad and Karen are back from church," she said, watching the sweep of car lights in the gravel driveway. Karen had gone to a Christmas program rehearsal.

Jumping up, Julie's mom filled the teapot with water, then put tea bags in two mugs. "Will you take Karen upstairs while I talk with your dad?"

Julie nodded. When Karen bounced inside, Julie volunteered to play "Candy Land," an offer she knew her little sister wouldn't refuse. Hand in hand, they raced upstairs. Closing her bedroom door, Julie said a silent prayer for her parents.

If her dad had a bleeding ulcer already, what in the world would *this* do to him?

An hour later, after tucking Karen in for the night, Julie closed the door to her own room. Standing at the card table, she put her parents out of her mind as she sorted through the remaining dozen puzzle pieces, covered with pink blotches and white lines.

She worked for a few minutes, arranging the pink and white pieces, until she had a white trellis covered with pink climbing roses attached to the cottage. At last the fishing village picture was complete.

"Too bad I can't arrange my *life* like a puzzle," Julie mumbled. "What can you do when some of the pieces are missing, and some just won't fit?"

At ten-thirty, Julie still lay wide awake in bed. Staring at the faint stars out her bedroom window, she took a deep breath and faced her feelings. Her worst fear had come true—they'd lost their home.

Now it was simply a matter of signing on the dotted line.

Scrimping and saving, cleaning the cafeteria for free lunches, helping with her mom's day care business, giving up cheerleading—none of it had made any difference at all. God still hadn't answered her desperate prayer to save their farm.

Julie's throat burned with unshed tears. It would feel good to release everything that had been bottled up inside her for weeks. She wanted to cry, to bury her face in her pillow and let the tears come. But she couldn't.

Staring up into the blackness, Julie sighed and let go of her pleading with God. Exhausted, she recalled the magnet on the refrigerator: "God gives the best to those who leave the choice to Him."

In spite of her deep disappointment, Julie knew she still trusted God. She'd have to let Him choose where they'd live. He'd provide them with a home somehow.

Monday was a "teacher in-service" day, so Julie was home in the afternoon when Mrs. Dann arrived. Since it was nap time, most of the children were asleep on beds, couches, and fold-out floor mats. Julie kept one ear tuned for the sound of crying babies as she stood in the dining room doorway.

The realtor and her parents sat around the table. Mrs. Dann's heavy gold bracelets jangled as she removed legal-sized documents from her briefcase, then spread them across the table.

"You'll need to sign here, here, and here." She handed Julie's dad a ball-point pen. "Yesterday the buyer gave me a check for the down payment. After the check clears and we take care of some legalities, we'll be able to close the deal."

"It happened so quickly." Julie's mom twisted her

wedding ring around and around her finger. "I guess it will take time to get used to the idea."

"I'll never get used to it." Julie's dad lunged forward, his hands clenched into fists. "This house has been in my family for three generations."

"I'm sure this is very difficult," Mrs. Dann sympathized. "However, I have some news that might help." She handed Mr. McGregor the buyer's down payment.

Julie shook her head. She couldn't imagine any news that could make losing their home easier. Even if the buyer had offered to pay them double their asking price, it wouldn't ease the pain of moving.

Her dad stared open-mouthed at the paper in his hand. "I don't understand. Why did Chuck Daniels write us a check?"

*"Monica's* dad?" Julie darted forward to peer over her dad's shoulder.

*"That's* my news!" Mrs. Dann beamed, her oversized teeth gleaming in her round face. "I understand Mr. Daniels used to be a neighbor of yours."

"Yes, before their divorce," Julie's mom agreed. "He lives in Elmwood now."

"I don't see much of him anymore," Julie's dad admitted, "but our families did things together when he was still married."

"Well, he mentioned that you'd been a very good friend to him once—something about a serious family problem?"

Eyes widening, Julie's dad nodded. "I remember," he said, but he didn't elaborate. Julie had no idea what he was talking about, and evidently her dad didn't intend to say.

Shrugging, Mrs. Dann went on. "Anyway, to repay you, he's buying your house and the acre it sits on. He hopes you'll continue to live here, while paying him rent." Mrs. Dann waved her hands in circles, grinning. "And this is the best part! He wants you to apply the rent payments toward repurchasing your home."

Confused, Julie looked from her parents back to Mrs. Dann. This sounded too good to be true. "You mean we can still live here, and buy back our house from Monica's dad, even though we lost the eighty arces?"

"That's about the size of it."

"I don't know what to say." Mr. McGregor gripped his wife's hand. "I mean—well, of course we'd like to stay. I'm sure I can still rent enough ground to farm."

"Then that's settled," Mrs. Dann said briskly. "I'll contact Mr. Daniels tonight and get things rolling. He'll be pleased that you've agreed to his plan. 'I always felt I owed him,' was the way he put it."

Just then one of the babies woke up, squalling. Julie's mom hurried to quiet the baby before he woke up everyone else. Mr. McGregor walked Mrs. Dann to her car. Julie sank down at the table, trying to absorb it all.

In a moment, her dad was back and joined her. "I still

can't believe it." He scratched his head. "Who would've guessed things might work out this way?"

Julie grinned. *"Mom* would have. She said all along that God would take care of us."

"I should have had the same confidence."

Julie traced the tablecloth pattern with her finger. "It sure will seem funny, paying Mr. Daniels for our house."

"It's not much different from other people who have bank mortgages on their homes. Instead of owing a bank, though, we'll pay Chuck a monthly rent."

Julie nodded, but inside she disagreed. This new arrangement was a *lot* different than having a bank own their house. Monica had ridiculed her badly enough for her secondhand clothes. Now she'd *really* give her a rough time. Julie braced herself for the next day, wincing at the knot of dread forming in her stomach.

Once Monica heard that her dad now owned the McGregors' house, she'd *never* let Julie hear the end of it.

*Chapter 10*

# *Second Chances*

Julie slept hard that night and awoke the next morning, surprised. For weeks she'd tossed and turned all night, and a solid night's sleep was rare.

Stretching out under her electric blanket, she peered at her clock's lighted dial—5:52 a.m. The alarm was set for six; no point in getting too cozy again.

Julie thought back over the previous day, but she still could hardly believe it. They wouldn't have to move after all! Her mom had been right all along. God *would* provide for their needs—and He certainly had in a surprising way.

The only drawback was that Monica's dad now owned their house. Julie knew Mr. Daniels had inherited a lot of money, and if he wanted to invest some of it in buying their home, she was grateful.

Still, she hated the idea of facing Monica's sarcastic comments on the bus that morning.

*Brr-r-r-r-ring!*

Julie rolled over and hit the alarm's "off" button. Shivering, she grabbed her school clothes and padded barefoot down the stairs. If she was lucky, she'd beat Karen to the heat vent in the dining room, the warmest spot in the house.

Standing above the heat register a moment later, the hot air made Julie's long granny pajamas balloon out. Silverware clinked and pans clunked in the kitchen, filling the morning with busy, *normal* sounds. Her dad was even whistling!

Leaning against the wall, Julie closed her eyes and breathed a sigh of relief.

An hour later the bus pulled to a stop at the end of their driveway, its brakes squealing. Snuggled down inside her wool scarf, Julie stomped her feet, then climbed aboard. "Hi, Bud," she said, as the doors closed behind her.

Plopping down in the seat beside Monica, Julie waited. Monica glanced at her, but said nothing. *This is a first,* Julie thought, her stomach churning. Why was Monica tongue-tied?

Monica cleared her throat. "Um, I'm sorry I mentioned to your mom that you quit the cheerleading squad. She asked how practices were going, and I said we missed you. I figured she already knew you'd dropped out."

"That's OK." Julie wondered what Monica was up to. Why didn't she say anything about owning their house?

"Personally," Monica continued, "I couldn't believe it when I heard you'd quit. How come?"

Julie took a deep breath. She might as well get it over with. "It was the money—for uniform rental and new shoes. I couldn't ask my parents for it when money was already so short."

"Is that why you also work in the cafeteria?"

"For free lunches." Julie stared at her lap, picking lint from her mittens. "I wanted to help out."

Monica was quiet for the next two miles as she drew smiley faces on the frost on the window. Sitting stiffly, Julie waited for the bomb to drop.

Finally Monica turned back to her. "I'm sorry about your money problems. Is that the real reason you're selling your house? I hate the idea that you might move. Has anyone looked at your house yet?"

Julie's eyes opened in surprise. Why was Monica hinting around, when she knew perfectly well her own dad had bought it?

"A few families have looked," Julie admitted cautiously.

Monica clutched Julie's arm. "You can't move! What'll I do without you?"

Julie frowned, studying Monica's face. Was this an act? She *seemed* genuinely upset. One by one, Julie peeled Monica's fingers from her arm.

"Well, don't have a fit yet."

Julie was relieved beyond measure that Monica didn't know her own father now owned the McGregors' house. Telling Monica shouldn't be a big deal, Julie knew, but she wasn't ready for her pride to take another beating yet.

After the transfer at Timmons Grove, Julie sat alone the rest of the way to school. Watching the black, plowed fields of dirt roll by, she became aware of nagging feelings of guilt in the back of her mind.

Julie knew that part of it was for lying to Monica about the house not being sold. However, Julie suspected that she was ashamed of herself for something more serious.

Julie had tried several times over the years to talk with Monica about her beliefs. She wanted her friend to know that God was the answer to *her* problems too—Monica's loneliness since the divorce, her feeling that no one really loved her.

And now Julie had a chance to share with Monica how God had answered the biggest prayer of her life—saving their home. Squirming in her seat, Julie knew she had no right to be embarrassed at the way God had answered her prayer.

Even so, she couldn't bring herself to tell Monica the truth. Monica would simply say that her own *dad* had answered Julie's prayer—not God.

At school that morning, Julie arrived in homeroom to find a summons to the principal's office. Julie hurried to the office and nervously knocked on Mrs. Oswald's private door. She hoped there hadn't been complaints about her work in the cafeteria.

"Come in."

Julie stepped inside and held out her summons.

"Oh, yes, I wanted to talk with you." Towering over Julie, Mrs. Oswald closed the door and pulled up an extra chair. "I got a call from your mother this morning."

Julie gasped. "What's wrong?" she asked, as a picture of her dad, bent over in pain, flashed through her mind.

"Nothing! I didn't mean to alarm you. Your mom called to ask about reinstating you on the cheerleading squad."

"She did?"

"Yes, she blames herself that you resigned without telling her. She said she would find the money for your outfit."

"It wasn't her fault," Julie mumbled. "I don't want her to feel guilty about the money. That's why I never told them in the first place."

"I understand," Mrs. Oswald assured her, "and I also admire your working in the cafeteria to pay for your school lunches." She tapped her pencil on the edge of the desk. "By the way, your mother knows about your job now. I mentioned the good job you were doing. I didn't know you hadn't told them at home. Your mom thought you were still carrying your lunch."

"I let her think so." Julie twisted her hands together in her lap. "Was she angry?"

"No, not at all. Just surprised." The principal hesitated. "And a bit hurt, too," she added gently. "You seem to have kept a lot of things to yourself lately."

Julie hung her head, feeling beaten. What could she say? It was true. She had worried about her dad not talking to anyone about his problems, yet Julie had figured she could handle *her* problems on her own.

"What did you tell her about the cheerleading?"

"The only thing I could—that your position had been filled already. Wendy Conklin was next in line, so she took your place."

"Oh." The wild hope that had soared for a moment fell with a thud. Julie started to rise.

Waving a hand, Mrs. Oswald motioned for her to sit back down. "I've thought it over, and if you agree, I'd like to name you First Alternate on the squad. You would attend all the practices and games, ready to fill in for anyone who is sick or can't make it for some reason."

Julie gripped her hands together to keep from clapping like a kindergartner. "It's a neat idea. Having a substitute *would* be helpful. I appreciate getting a second chance."

"I'm glad we could work it out," Mrs. Oswald said. "Before you go, can I give you a bit of advice?"

"Sure."

"Don't keep your problems to yourself from now on.

Bottling up troubles only makes them worse. I know you wanted to spare your parents more worry, and I admire that. But *do* talk to someone. I'm here if you need me, and I know your mother really cares about you."

Julie nodded. Then, shaking the principal's hand, she left the office and headed back to class.

All morning Julie felt like pinching herself to make sure she wasn't dreaming. She couldn't wait for the next practice. Having a "first alternate" on the cheerleading squad could be very important, she decided. God had answered this prayer, too, in an unexpected way.

The rest of the week flew by, with two cheerleading practices sandwiched into Julie's crowded schedule. Using some of the day care money, Julie's mom bought her the cheerleading shoes, with the understanding that they were an "early Christmas present." Julie agreed eagerly. Just getting back on the squad was Christmas present enough for her.

On Friday evening Julie packed her birthday gift, grabbed her duffel bag, sleeping bag, and pillow, then piled everything into the car. Eight girls would be at Monica's, and Julie was grateful not to be left out.

The Daniels' circle drive was jammed with cars. Six girls were already there, and Heather arrived as Julie's dad drove away. They went inside together. Between the blaring stereo and the chattering girls, the volume was already deafening.

"Happy birthday!" Julie shouted, handing Monica her package.

Monica added Julie's present to the jumbled pile in the middle of the family room floor. Julie tossed her coat on the couch, then stacked her pillow, duffel bag, and sleeping bag in the corner.

"Presents first!" Monica yelled above the noise. Folding herself gracefully onto the floor, she spread the gifts around her. Julie and the others sat cross-legged in a semicircle to watch.

One by one, Monica ripped open the boxes, "oohing" and "ahhing" over each gift. From Heather, June, and Theresa came a board game, earrings, and a sweater. From Andrea, Erin, and Sandi she received a hooked rug kit, some paperback joke books, and a giant box of fancy chocolates.

Julie squirmed as Monica reached for her box. Her gift was the only handmade present in the group.

Monica tore off the glittery bow and paper, then lifted the plump, pink chenille bear from the box. "Oh, look!" She held the bear for everyone to see. "I love stuffed animals! Thanks, Julie!"

Andrea leaned close. "I'd like one myself. Where did you buy it?" she asked Julie. "Did they have other colors?"

Chewing her lip, Julie stared at the bear. How could she admit to her friends that her gift was made from a piece of old, threadbare bedspread?

"Um, I saw some bears like this at the new craft store in the mall." Then, recalling her mom's words about the Lord providing the idea, Julie stumbled on. "I didn't buy the bear, though. I made it myself." Julie waited for the snickers, but they didn't come.

Andrea studied the bear closely. "You really made this? Did you sew on the face and everything?"

Julie nodded. "It's stuffed with cotton balls and old pantyhose."

Erin smiled at that. "Could you show us how to sew one? They'd make neat Christmas presents."

Surprised, Julie nodded. "I just cut a pattern out of a paper sack. You could make whatever size you like." Julie glanced at Monica. "I could go get the rest of that pink bedspread, then show everybody how to make the bears. I mean, if you want me to. It's your party."

"Why not? We could work on the bears while we watched a movie." Monica pointed to all her gifts and passed around the box of candy. "Thanks, everybody!"

Julie went in the kitchen to call home. When she asked about the bedspread, her mom offered to bring it over, along with some embroidery floss. "Say, do you want those two pillows that are coming apart? You could remove the stuffing and use it for your bears."

"Sure! And thanks, Mom." Julie hung up and joined the party.

After devouring four medium pizzas, the eight girls gathered around Monica's large dining room table to cut the chenille bedspread into bear shapes. Julie could hardly believe it as she watched her friends talking and joking while they sewed the various-sized bears.

As the night wore on, the noise died down somewhat. Monica's mom and sister went up to bed. As the bears were finished, they were lined up along the top of the couch—some laughing, some serious, and one with big tears sewn running down its face.

At midnight, Julie propped her pillow against the fireplace, then snuggled partway down into her sleeping bag to watch the movie. At two a.m. the movie ended, and Monica turned out the lights. Yawning, Julie slid flat to the floor, burrowing into her pillow.

At first all was quiet. Then Julie heard soft voices whispering back and forth. In the still night, the faint words were clear.

Haltingly, Erin asked Monica several questions about her parents' divorce, admitting that her own parents had just split up too. Julie's stomach hurt at the pain in Erin's voice. She'd laughed with the others all evening, and Julie had never guessed anything was wrong.

Other voices whispered other secrets then, sharing in the dark what they'd hidden earlier. Theresa was sure that her older sister was taking drugs, but she'd been warned not to tell. June's brother had run away from home, but had been found hiding in a park. June sounded terrified that he would try it again. Sandi confided that her grandfather had cancer and wasn't expected to live until Christmas.

Heather reached over and poked Julie's arm. "Did you hear all that?" she whispered.

"I heard." Julie leaned closer to Heather's dark form. "I had no idea everybody else had such awful problems."

But then, Julie realized, few people knew *her* family was having trouble either. As Mrs. Oswald had pointed out, she didn't talk much about her worries. Evidently most of her friends didn't either.

The longer she lay there and listened, the more Julie ached for her friends. So many of them sounded scared.

In her heart, Julie knew that God wanted to help her friends, just as He'd helped Julie's family. But unless she told them, would her friends even know where to turn? She didn't think many of them even went to church.

Julie longed to help. And yet . . .

She had no desire to be ridiculed. Just because they hadn't made fun of her homemade chenille bear didn't mean they wouldn't laugh if she talked to them about God.

Lying in the dark, hearing about her friends' struggles, Julie knew she had no choice. True, some of the girls might laugh, but it would be wrong not to share how God had cared for her. Julie knew how it felt to be alone and scared in the night.

Taking a deep breath, she said, "Monica?" Her voice sounded loud in the quiet darkness. "Are you awake, Monica?"

"Yeh? What's up?"

Julie knew the others could hear too, but she pushed on. "You know how we've been having money problems at home. Well, we've had some really neat answers to prayer about it."

"Answers to prayer?" Monica asked, her tone skeptical.

Heart pounding, Julie forced herself to go ahead. "Mom said all along that we could trust God to help us, but I had trouble believing that for awhile. She was right, though."

Heather reached over in the dark, found Julie's hand, and squeezed it. Feeling more brave, Julie squeezed back, glad for the support.

"You know my cafeteria job that pays for my school lunches? That was one answer. So was finding a way to make you a present so I could come to the party."

Monica sniffed. "What about your house? When somebody buys it, you'll have to move."

Julie closed her eyes a moment. "Actually, somebody already *did* buy our house. It turned out to be another answer to prayer."

"How do you figure that?" Monica demanded, thrashing

noisily in her nylon sleeping bag. “When did this happen? You can’t move!”

“Wait a minute!” Julie raised her voice above the sudden eruption of questions. “We don’t have to move after all. Monica, *your* dad bought our house. We’ll keep living there and pay him rent. We might even buy it back sometime.”

*“My* dad owns *your* house?” Monica squealed. “Really? I can’t believe it!” She chuckled. “Last week I told him about your sack lunches and secondhand clothes, but I didn’t tell him your house was for sale. I wonder how he knew?”

“It isn’t important,” Julie said. “The only thing that matters is that God says He’ll take care of us if we trust Him, and He will.”

Julie breathed a huge sigh of relief. The news about their house was out, yet no one had laughed. More importantly, she’d let her friends know that there was Someone who cared about the hurts in *their* lives too, Someone who wanted to help them.

Yawning, Julie yanked her zipper up and rolled over. Snuggling down in her cozy sleeping bag, warmth spread through her as she drifted off to sleep.